Chronicle of an English Morpheme Addict

{Being the Third Tale in A Measure of Poe & Three Quarters}

Steven Mooney

Steven Mooney Books
Olympia, Washington

ISBN: 978-1-7345356-8-6
Library of Congress Control Number: 2020905158
Cover Art & Design by Jessica Bell Design
Published by Steven Mooney Books

For Dina

There is no word that is not the best in some place. Consequently, however low it be, however unusual, poetic, archaic, new, obsolete, harsh, barbarous, and exotic, nevertheless, let it be placed in its own company…so that if ever a need for it arise, it may be summoned then.

– Desiderius Erasmus of Rotterdam

Book One

The Auction Block Romance

That morning I dawdled at crosswalks and kiosks reluctant to meet a repeat client and again treat her serpentine temblors, yet the cadence of the crowd carried me along and I fell in with the rumble-mumble of our urban lingua franca, a vocal collage of all things morphemic while I pondered the numerous times when I had seemingly cured this woman's addictive fix, ever a preamble to a concomitant, roosting jones. Then the thought struck: could Ratatat Haha be addicted to the treatment? A Stockholm Syndrome of the syllabic?

As I made my way up the street, pacing the inevitable, I reviewed there was no greater puzzle than a repeat client who defied scientific laws and the sharpest conjectures of the best minds of her generation yet was clearly afflicted; it was a conundrum of the age for which the field was teething for results. The elevator doors opened and I was greeted by my colleague Melody.

"Morning, you've got Haha waiting in three and Mrs. Mannhein in two."

"She's here already? I don't mind them coming early, but three hours?"

"She said, wait I scribbled it, she said: 'this room is the only spot of harmonious convergence in the tri-state area.' Maybe it's the wallpaper."

"Have you checked on her?"

"Which her do you mean? You may remember that she's conflicted, but then so is Haha."

"Whose confliction is the question. Since when did Dusenburg become Mannheim?"

"I don't see disunity in Haha, but merely the *trans* in transgender."

"Should I make tea?"

It was another of our jousts; when she had no clients and played secretary, she was quickly bored with the mundane of the routine, or did I have that backwards, and felt compelled to enliven our work space with an array of word games, as had been her want since she had come to work with me, and it was she who'd supplied an in-house moniker following each client's initial visit. For example, Ratatat Haha had acquired her *nom de mimique* from the point of her inaugural addiction: the free morpheme *ha* uttered in a repetitious staccato tic that carried the echolalic popping of a burp gun. Mumbling a few words of the sort, give me strength oh beacon in the twilight, I tapped on the door and stepped inside. Dr. Fordham was seated at the table, fingers laced.

"Hello Wallis, it's a pleasure to see you again."

She gave me a tightlipped smile that seemed to crack open her narrow face, one in transition from…well she'll make a handsome woman. But she had checked the grin, for excess glee put her at risk, as well she knew.

"I wanted to tell you in person, Randal, that at long last I have traced my family."

"This is exceptional news!"

"As you are aware, I had ceased answering the, well, you know, (among her previous morphemic bleats were *telephone* and its freebase *phone*) and then one day there was a card and then another and I learned she, my sister is—back here now, and I will see her, well, all of them very soon." She held up a hand when I started to speak.

"I can assure you that none of them carry any of my associations; there is no genetic link. I know you will say that we have yet to examine the angle malaprop or some such, but I just *feel* so much more relaxed, like her presence unwound the spring in my head, or whatever it is."

"And with the therapy, you are maintaining our schedule, I presume?"

"Well, I can assure you I haven't had a wisecrack in weeks, no puns, snappy comebacks, nothing."

"Are you back teaching or in the lab?"

"I've extended the sabbatical, but I am writing again!"

"Well, just be careful, try to keep everything on the narrow, and don't range too far afield of the basic descriptive; I needn't remind you there are minefields lurking in the compound-complex sentence structures strewn with dependent clauses. I believe we have learned through our sessions that specific pieces of your research are not in themselves caution signs, for example when we analyzed that piece that compared the Elizabethan fleur-de-lis to the street grid of Stratford-on-Avon; and it turned up nothing new. Rather, it is the nature of the language to be invasive that is the truest culprit and—"

"Culprit… culprit!"

"Easy now, of course, varlet would be a more accurate term, given your field."

"Culprit *is* rather plebian, whereas *vaarlet*, hmm, a lovely bilabial: *varlet* rolls nicely, varlet, varlet, varlet, varlet, varlet, varlet, varleh, var-huh, var-huh, vhuh-huh-huh-huh—"

"That's it, remember our rhythmic: *breathe deep the see saw, breathe deep the see saw; in and out, in and out, con-cen-trate on breath-ing*, there you go, the inhale and the exhale, recall the harmonium, nice and easy. Nice and—okay, that was close."

"Oh… okay, but… such lovely syllables… what do you mean by close? Why, you set me up! I've noted before the holes in your therapy."

"Doctor Fordham, as we have both acknowledged today and at other times, it is the nature of the language to be invasive, and given that construct we are at risk at every waking moment; I would posit that we are all morpheme addicts to one extent or another, it is how we handle our varied urges and purges that makes all the difference: look at what we did with that hallmark of egregious denunciation, that disbelieving smirk of yours that rhymed with Rah! We took it head on; that you have had a wandering streak of others just as plaintive makes our commitment all the stronger. But if you'd like to switch to Ms. Ungwen, then please do so."

"Well, you see, ah—"

"Just now, did you attack by anaphora, trailing the clutch morpheme with a noun or noun phrase? Do you remember our work with *mad* world, *mad* kings!? Or did you enfilade by epistrophe, as we have also done, stringing along the line and planting the clutch at the end? Well? It is hardly realistic to call into question my approach, one based on solid methodology, when you abandon our work outright and lurch at, at—"

"*Lurch*, how lovely a verb to move onward with your treatment, Doctor Poe, but at the same time I think I will give your colleague a try, get a double shot going, from both east and west as it were, and with my family back together, well, I want to thank you, anyway."

When she was gone, I sat awhile. Let Dusenburg wait, she hasn't been here in ages. I ruminated on the bumpy road I'd traveled with one patient and that now it may have forked with her perchance spilling out into the maelstrom from which she had come, into the oral spasms of consonant clusters and vowel streams, out among the bound and free morphemes of English, a turbulent caterwaul of the oral/aural, an absolute avalanche of onomatopoeia. I decided then to forego protocol and to advance the weekend.

"Mrs. Dusenburg, how nice to see you again," I said, the tone drooling floorward as my jaw dropped. A man in his skivvies sat amid a pile of clothing.

"Hi Doc, well that get up is just too hot, you know. I tried opening the window, how about some AC in here."

It took me a moment to come alive. It wasn't as though he had been in drag that was so startling but that, well, up to then he really had looked like a woman, the real thing, and not remotely like the man who sat before me.

"It's a New York summer and AC is doing what it can Mrs. Ah, is it Mr. Dusenburg?"

"It doesn't matter, does it? Where I've been you could be either or both or something else entirely."

"I don't know where to begin," I said.

"Adjectives are a good bet."

"Okay, so regardless of the exterior, the interior needs are the same. But I wonder if there's perhaps a contradiction that unsettles what may be seen as, shall we say, balance?"

"Now doc, don't be sexist. I have a thousand and one faces, but that doesn't alter the need I have to get rid of this age-old impulse that has followed me down the centuries like a witch."

Well, the gift of metaphor hadn't changed, nor had the Elizabethan-tinted English accent. In like fashion she, well whoever, had through the course of treatment described a condition somewhat similar to but diverse from Tourette's syndrome, developed at an early age. I swiveled and opened the file and reviewed that we had covered the known bases of the vocalic Tourette's martyr that include (but are not limited to) grunting, barking, uttering words or phrases and even echolalia, the copy-cataloging of another's speech, but few patterns addressed the common ailment of your garden variety morpheme addict, that of repetitive utterance, wherein a singular devotion to a select morpheme is given a debilitative focus like that of a broken record. Who remembers broken records? I'd had to look it up. But now I know! Dusenburg had (I would drop the gender complement if there were to hand a satisfactory replacement) yet to relate the earliest fixation with adjectives, but I believed herm or shem (see what I mean?) to be a dead ringer for one afflicted since childhood; s/he bore many signs of the neurobehavioral truant what with inattentiveness and impulsivity; when s/he paid attention to me, s/he couldn't sit still, but when s/he eased into a chair, s/he was off somewhere else entirely. Yet, s/he was unlike many other patients in that addiction wasn't limited to vocal representation. S/he had that of course, and in one of our early sessions had demonstrated how well joined were the bilabial consonants and alveolar fricatives when she conveyor-belted a bevy of yelped *all* while tittuping about like a flustered emu. I have seen other patients ring off like that with polymorphemic words and come away thinking they'd created a neologism that had freed them from their enslavement, and they would run or jump or want to go airborne with their discovery, and it always broke my heart a little bit to give them the sad news that they had merely squirmed into one end of a semantic tube and crawled out the other. No, Dusenburg was also, apparently, a morpheme collector. Today, he brought from his pocket a rectangle of crinkly foolscap.

"See it here: t'is a mite age affected, knurled by monks, but clearly an *all* made from a quill… hmmm, aquill? A quill, aquill, quill, quill. Nah, not to my taste," and he gave me that leer-like grin where one side of her mouth rolled up toward an ear as a lock of raven mane descended.

"Wait, before we move on here, I need to know something, and a name will do. That way we can avoid gender discrimination within the limits of case," I said.

"Fair enough, I'm kind of stuck on *Claudia* if you must know, and have been for eons, tee hee."

"Okay, Claudia it is. So, Claudia, I don't aim to be too skeptical, but you know my credo," and I waved a hand toward the framed copy of the oath of the practitioner of the field, an iamb- enjambed encomium loosely parsed from the Hippocratic Oath in Occidental font.

"So, while it's important to do no harm, I must be truthful: there is no telling where this scrap came from; it is way too small to provide clues as to its origin, and I just don't want to see you taken."

"I appreciate your honesty counselor because it tells me you really care, but this is no ordinary *all*: this is a rather special piece of paper."

"You didn't ah, in the absence of a sticky-note, tear it off of the corner of a document?"

She stood and began pacing, and I imagined some illuminated manuscript besmirched, a statue missing a limb.

"It's freezing in here," said Claudia, "have you got something I can wear?" I was about to suggest the dress she came in but shook my head and left the room. I needed to move my legs and swivel my head and do some breathing of my own. Besides, I thought there was an old sweatshirt in a back closet.

"How is she today?" said Melody.

"She's a he today, best I can tell," and I went on past the lobby and into the kitchen for a glass of orange juice and then went to rummage in the closets. When I came back through, Melody stood beside the elevator doors, arms akimbo.

"Did I miss someone?" She turned and took the sweats and tossed them on a chair.

"Now, you tell me," she said, "when she came up earlier today, she was wearing a floor-length-velvet Kelly burnoose, but just now she had on a mauve outfit with a skirt that's a little short for a woman her age, and she wasn't blond. What is going on?" In the treatment room we found the green outfit along with shoes and nylons, but no wig. We stood there confabulating scenario, and as we gathered up Dusenburg's shroud-like garment something rang the déjà vu doorbell while Melody did that feminine thing of holding up each item and measuring it against some innate algebra before folding them while I turned my attention to that onionskin fragment, seemingly more crinkled in that now calved slivers lay curled on the table. I opened the curtains for better light. As I reached for the shard, it seemed to brown and wither as from heat and when my fingers closed it crumbled to dust with a faint but musty odor.

In the lobby I found Melody packing up to go home, seemingly unconcerned about the day's events, and yet she was puttering so she had something to say. I knew that if I left the room and went to my office that she wouldn't follow but would let me know through telepathy that something was on her mind. It had happened many times before; she often seemed on the brink of thinking my thoughts for me. So, I puttered as well. Finally, she picked up her bag and at the elevator, turned.

"Are you still planning to go to that morpheme auction at Boothby's on Saturday?"

"Oh yeah, absolutely, thanks for the reminder; I might have forgotten again."

"Well, I can't go with you. I know I said I would, and I really wanted to see what they put on the block, what they use for a block, but Justin called from Cornell and he can get away this weekend and if we don't it's going to be turkey day before I see him."

"Hey, no probs, I'm happy for you, really. Look, it's going to be a weathered, leather-skinned crowd there, putting up all manner of fuss and flapdoodle when it comes to the bidding, and I'll just shorthand the notes, so hey, have fun and we'll see you back here bright but not early Monday." The elevator's whoosh approached.

"You don't *know* shorthand," she laughed, as the elevator opened its maw.

"It's the longhand version." I went back to my office with thoughts of those musty crumbs left by Claudia Dusenburg, or whoever she was, when my eye caught the calendar and the big star that I'd drawn on the 14th— our anniversary! Leaning the chair back I drifted to our founding days, back when English as an international language had met the digital age corpus of acronyms and net lingo and wingdings in the rush-hour traffic of those ever changing -isms and -ologies of a post-modern world, a time when new highways emerged: phono-morphology, at once jeered by linguistics and constructivist pathology as an autistic urchin, faux clown and pretender to the therapy throne of an unrecognized –ism, yet amid the jockeying of doctrines for pole position at the start of a new millennium, phomorphs, as we were (dis)affectionately known, gained respect due to our unalterable faith in the interiority of our clients through the imaginary reconstitution of their personal narrative (oft gone awry), for psychopathology had to that time rather unsuccessfully treated the imbalance of sequencialization of the transitory hyperbolic, for one.

Now, as a resident here for a number of years, I've encountered just about everything sex-wise under the lexical sun, but Claudia Dusenburg took the Blue Ribbon, though I didn't see gender articulated in her narrative plot; for I have seen cross dressers, treated some with gender pronoun issues, and I've seen transvestites too, they being harder to miss, to flag the old pun, and none of them spoke for this *model*; I marveled at the word while searching the brain banks for a better one. A transgender, concluded, but how does that explain the pecs and that walk, strutting around the room: that was a guy: I got nowhere with it; a woman arrived, became a guy, and departed a woman, end of tale? Well, I had Dusenburg's phone number and email, so I'd delve into it later. Looking back on it, I both did but didn't, as events would tell.

2

As I stepped from a taxi, I was swarmed by the early morning session spilling into the blazing heat, some stringing down the taxi stand, still others in abandon, yet more huddled in heroic knots while brandishing trophy. Finding no egress in that melee, I wiggled left when the trailing foot of an admorph swiped my side. "Hey, watch it with that *ate*," I yelled! Turning, I spied a gap and raced up the stairs and charged into the foyer undilated-eye-blind and collided with someone who went *ooff* and we went tumbling over entangled, and that's how I met another Claudia, but this one so much the Real McCoy that for a time I forgot about the other.

"It is such an awkward and abrupt transition, darling, you really must engage in your writing class. Besides," she said, "you're omitting the Pomeranian and those tins, not to mention how it really happened."

"Like I said before, I thought the dog was yours? It's a fossilized memory, left out on purpose."

"If it had been mine and you kicked it, we wouldn't be having this conversation. As it were, you nearly got us crushed in that avalanche of Del Monte," she said.

"You're right we wouldn't be together if you had a thing like that, call it a dog if you want, but who would have guessed that bouffant rat was harnessed to a pyramid of fruit cocktail," I said, again unable to recall a dog, but I'd kept up the pretense because jousting with her was better than with Melody, for Claudia's *English* lopped off final consonants and sliced the tips off vowels like radishes!

"*Vintage* fruit cocktail no less, the brochure mentioned the pantry of a sealed bomb shelter in Edinburgh Castle. All that vacuum-packed fructose outlasted the V-2s, not to mention the rest of the century. And if you're going to tell this tale, then make it right and proper. I won't have my good name smeared again" she said, twirling the opera glasses with the broken swivel that she kept around for God knows why: they made a nice paperweight, and the inlaid pearl was curio perfect, but otherwise they were worthless crap, like I didn't have enough of already.

She strolled off.

Then, when I thought of a great line and walked into her room to add the rejoinder, she wasn't there. I hadn't heard her leave, and I stood perplexed in Venetian shafts of light as swirling dust motes measured egress, but whose, not the teddy bears and odd knickknacks she'd gathered from across the pond. I picked up the glasses and twirled them and the swivel's metallic snick reminded me of my writing teacher's walk, mincing steps in stilettos is what you get with your eyes closed, but otherwise he's a balding ovoid nearing sixty.

On Claudia's insistence, I took up this course: *Fiction for the Compleat Novice*; in order to satisfy her ambulant determination that I would know how to record the events that followed from our impromptu entanglement on Bootheby's tiles, regardless of a life in writing and the chronicles of its adventures. But why fiction, you may wonder, when, upon reading what follows you'll conclude, as surely you must, the elements of this story are as factual as the nose on your face; add to that a career in journalism *before* I went to college and earned a somewhat august set of degrees. Well, the answer is it boils down to reported speech. Before and since I met Claudia, I've spent more time in *listening* (the better twin of *speaking*) than I would have thought possible for a middle-aged guy without golf shoes (a footnote to my dad and porkers like him who hit the links to chew the fat; but that's another story). Anyway, how to write dialogue?

In journalese we quote it, and in gonzo cases paraphrase, but it ain't the same beast. First off, there has to be *tension*; you can't have your wife and daughter agreeing with each other over devilled eggs, or your dad and his bone-head brother admiring how nice the lawn looks. Then there's pacing, another blob of tense, not verb tense; it's like the way you'd lead a monster from a cavern with a taste of blood: your blood.

So, I'm putting all of that in and then next week or the one after I'll show it to the class and they'll critique it while the Ovoid arranges his beret and lights another Gauluois. But they're not going to like it, they're going to squirm and fidget like they always do, especially the plump front row: When you note that right angle perspective upon entering the classroom, they do resemble a line of stuffed chair models posing at a furniture expo. Almost everybody in this fiction class is puffy. I've lain awake pondering puff because the Ovoid (Chamois of the bantam beret) arranges things to catch our attention and alter our perception.

But what my classmates aren't going to like ought to be right up Chamois's alley, to pen a truly awful metaphor, and I'll get to all that after I bring you up to speed. You'll notice that Claudia has a famous name when I call your attention to it. I didn't learn it quite so simply, as our introduction was abbreviated and clumsy like a dryer-load of clothing tumbled out. What I did learn about her in that initial moment was of a ripe vocabulary and legs that went from here to Sunday. My eyes adjusted from bright sunlight amid a clatter of cans, a cursing lady and a yelping canine with its fur in curlers (supposedly).

While helping her to her feet, I apologized in three languages before introducing myself, as Bootheby's staff was giving me the eye, but instead she offered a hand with lavender lacquered nails.

"I'd have told you to bugger off if not for the politesse," she said.

"I've got a Thesaurus with that name," I said.

"So have I."

I fetched her bag and handed it to her.

"He was my grandfather," she said, smoothing her skirt, as I tried to focus on the British accent, but couldn't resist the eye candy wondrous anatomy beneath the sultry voice.

"So, how many *greats* removed would he be?"

"Oh, perhaps cubed, I can't remember. Like most folks, I know him more as a product than a person. But when I was a child, we had to memorize the title. Do you know it?" she said.

"In college we called it the book of Syn," I said.

"You Yanks. It's *Roget's Thesaurus of English Words and Phrases, Classified and Arranged so as to Facilitate the*

Expression of Ideas and Assist in Literary Composition. But I suppose you're preoccupied with *frontier*," she said.

"You Brits, that's a book in itself; you'd need a folio just for the title." But with a smile the counter jab fell just right, and before I left that day, I had her phone number. I spent the rest of the day carefully rolling vowels and imaging myself as a Jude Law type, utterly forgetting to take notes toward potential new clients, and when I put in my bid on the *-ing* I sounded like a dipthong-challenged cracker doing dinner theater Cockney.

While the superannuated morphemes (new ones are forever being coined, you know) stage of the auction went through its list (vintage fruit cocktail), I kept one eye on Ms. Roget. She was more expressive and less prim than I'd have expected from a Brit, but then it's always good medicine to have our stereotypes overhauled: pry open the maw of prejudice and go at the teeth with channel locks and a ball peen hammer. She got pretty excited over the bound morphemes, and particularly the lot of esses, but as each one was carted out for display, she sat back, diminished with each sale, yet she didn't bid at all but rather she seemed to sink in on herself, discouragement drawn on her like eye liner. Whatever it was that she had come to bid on went by her or wasn't there. And I had lost out, too. Perhaps she left that day wanting her -ess, if that was it, and I'd missed my -ing.

"You cannot put that in a story, not in this class you can't," said Chamois.

"So, slang is to be avoided altogether?" said one of the front row tubs.

"Slang, dear children," chided the beret, "is the vulgar lingo of the street; it is the underbelly of our language; it carries pathos like a pox. Your characters will be maligned and viewed in the pejorative, regardless of how they may otherwise shine."

Oh boy, I thought, he's really steamrolling this one. He's gonna flatten this one out and land planes on it. I wonder if what he's really saying is that he secretly admires informal language but is too chickenshit to use it. Chamois may be a published writer, but that doesn't purify his tap water, and that got me to thinking about fable and how you had to read between the lines if you wanted to have any fun. Like the goose that laid the golden egg: was it just gold on the outside? If the yolk was gold too, did that mean gilded cholesterol and what about the white? I was getting into it and prying up the floorboards to peek underneath when Chamois loomed again, waving what I knew had to be my story. I thought of heading him off with a rhetorical query into female slang and what a different sort of bird it is when he slapped the pages on my desk.

"Our Mr. Poe seems to think that every character is a backwater hick," he said.

No, just in your family, I thought.

"He has everyone sounding like everyone else; they are carbon copies of each other," he said, showing his age.

Carbon copies were used on the original typewriters in Ancient Greece. That's how the Pleiades were formed, and of course the conveyor belts down at the Zeus Nymph Factory had them on scrolls. Well, he didn't like the opening because he didn't know it was one, I crowed to myself. It was characterization that he couldn't get past his prejudices to appreciate. But then humility whispered that more likely it contained elements of what he'd been teaching against, what they castigate you for in MFA programs. I'd have to tear it up and start over, perhaps from the point of the burglary.

3

The following day, Sunday, was to be the auction's finale that would begin with the remaining items up for bid, and then with all unsold items going on the block at reduced rates. I called Claudia, mentioned again how sorry I was for the collision, but grateful that I had met such a charming and intelligent woman, and could I take her to dinner. Her reply held the dinner thing open for now but her tone implied yes, and offered to share a taxi that morning. I learned on the job that meant ride together, not fare share, but that was only the beginning of a day on which I, or rather we, would pay dearly.

I battled it out with an antiquarian bidder in a Wyatt Earp string bowtie right up to the eyebrows of my checking account, but by golly I got my *–ing.* I also got to know Claudia better; she sat with me the entire time and we carried on in whispers. Then, I over-dawdled our parting but at last got her a cab in pouring rain. She was headed uptown. Getting my own cab was a rain dance; I could have swum home faster.

When I arrived, soaking wet, I found my place had been trashed and I just stood there in the doorway like a brain-dead bellboy. I'd been given the Oscar Madison surprise, as it's known in cop jargon as one told me as he wrote his report on what was left of my desk. When they'd gone, I sat amid the rip rap of what had been the boulders of my cave. Beret was on to something. I really did need a lot of practice. My meditation on the trash parallel, the forced marriage of awful and offal, was interrupted by the phone, and I was surprised I still had one.

"Randal, is that you? It's Claudia. I've been trying to reach you!"

"Hi, yes, ah I've been out," I fumbled. Out is right, out in the shambles of memory lane.

"I need to speak with you," she said.

"Well, we can meet—"

"Randal, this is urgent, please! There's no one else I could call. Give me your address."

I surveyed the chaos and found a laughable symmetry in the Jackson Pollock of my new living room, and invited her over.

The first thing she said when I opened the door was, "You too?"

I offered her a glass of wine from a bottle I'd found, Chateau de Rummage, and we sat on the flaccid remains of throw pillows and commiserated. She'd arrived home after the auction (as I had) to find her belongings, her life, and her identity, strewn like confetti.

"It's as though I awoke from a dream then," she said, "and saw at once the grand façade of furnishings, that beneath the Corinthian leather and silk brocade was just, just—"

"A foam rubber sandwich," I said.

"It's funny how pretensions veil attitude," I waxed. "That which portrays a sirloin exterior, masks a corndog within. The world's greatest artwork hangs on sheetrock, and we never think about Shakespeare going to the toilet, but he did." But despite my flippancy, I was growing despondent, wayward in the squalor of my illusions amid the trappings of a plastic gentility where I pined for a dignity greater than the Styrofoam peanut. Claudia unstuck my hand from my brow and held it.

"This is all most odd, but then I think, is it really?" she said.

"How do you mean?"

"I'm not sure, exactly. Maybe I'm grabbing at straws," she said.

"There's some over there in the lampshade."

"Be serious, please. Tell me, what drew you to the auction?"

"Well, I was bequeathed a morpheme and went there looking for another one so I'd have a matched set," I said.

"Whatever for, I don't see your point," she said.

"Well, there's not much you can do with one *-ing*. Your choices are really limited," I said, not telling her all. I'd never explained it before, and it came out sounding pleonastic.

"You have limited yourself, I believe," she said.

Somehow, we had scooted closer and she hadn't objected to my arm around her; she'd snuggled in.

"Did you ever try inverting the "n"? Topsy-turvy it makes a "u," she said.

"That's amazing. I never considered it," I said.

"Now can't it thirty degrees and slip the "i" before the "g," what do you have?"

"Wow! All those years and I never saw it," I said.

"Oh please, Randal darling, once you set limits you end up caught inside them," she said. "The particles can be fun, or even risky."

"Risky," I said, recalling the range of emotion she displayed at the auction. It was like watching an actress mime a role. That's what Chamois said we should do with our own characters if it helps bring them from whole cloth to fruition, and there went attention span as the clothing image sent me down an alley where babushkas flirted with busbies and tartan argued with plaid and a kepi wrote its memoirs of the troubles in Djibouti.

"Was risk what brought you to Boothby's?" I asked.

"It's a long story, can it wait until tomorrow?"

"Everything can wait until tomorrow," I said.

"Not quite everything," she said, and led me through the clutter to my bedroom where it looked like a tornado had had a bad dream.

"Since you have no couch and I no home, this will have to do for tonight," she said, as we cleared away debris.

"I expect you to be every inch a gentleman."

"Every inch," I smiled back, and offered her my toothbrush.

4

The next morning after showering and cleaning up the bathroom, we started on the kitchen but gave in after running headlong into what might be called the pathos of the mop. The trick was not to take it seriously, but we wouldn't learn that until we cleaned her place. For now, we agreed that a café would fix us up nicely, so we went out and found one.

"We'll have tea and scones and an order of rashers," I said.

"Excuse me?" said the waitress.

"Randal."

"I want a British breakfast." Claudia ordered for us, and while we ate, she gave me the lowdown on her involvement with morphemes, and it rang Chamois chimes.

If I really wanted to rumple Chamois's feathers I'd begin this on a dark and stormy night, and it may have been, but I know it can't be done, and not just for the redundancy, but there *are* stormy nights. What to do? Stories ought to have intermissions, like plays. When you're writing along and you feel a stormy night approaching that may lead to swabbing linoleum strewn with refrigerator spew in dishware shards, pull the curtains, and head for the green room where history awaits with a sketch which I seemed to be attached to though I had no recall of its production.

Samuel Chase, Secretary of the Treasury in the Lincoln administration had by 1864 determined a final motto to inscribe U.S. one and two cent coins. For several years his office had wrangled with pious appeals received from their devout constituency: *In God We All Hold Trust* was eventually whittled away to *In God We All Trust*, and then finally shortened to its current form, the *All* having been sheared from the inscription and later presented to Claudia's illustrious grandfather for his inclusive and seminal work, much the rage of polite society since its publication. But it is the origin of that particular and significant morpheme that lies at the heart of this *tale*, as Chamois would have it, but I prefer *rendering*.

Chase, privileged to the president's ear yet mindful of it too beweighted, determined not to dawdle over pleasantries.

"Sir, I have a request to make, and within it is the kernel of an idea." The president nodded and waved him to a chair.

"If you'll recall, sir, that little word you gave to me, to my department, that we would place it upon the coinage, well sir, we have elected to withdraw it."

"Salmon, it is yours to do with as you wish," said the president.

"Lord Lyons has recently spoken of his last visit home, during which he met the distinguished Doctor Peter Mark Roget."

"The author of our good friend, the Thesaurus," said the president.

"Indeed, sir, not a day goes by that we don't use it. Why, that one book marks little time on the shelf. To show our appreciation, I would like to present Dr. Roget with the idle *all.*"

"One not to be included in the next edition, I presume," said the president.

"That would not be in the spirit of the gift, I believe it should stand alone," said Chase.

"Then let us do our duty to bestow upon it the condition of an honorarium."

"Splendid, Mr. President, I'll leave you then, and thank you."

Before Mr. Lincoln could reply, Chamois folded his arms across his chest and clucked, always a hopeful sign. He laid my work on the podium and then praised the use of historical figures in fiction without directly referring to me, but by now I knew him well enough not to expect it. He kept us all on a tether of expectation sprinkled with a modicum of tribute, but as always followed by a caution; in this case it was the assumed absence of nineteenth century collocation, and with it the implication that I hadn't done my homework. Until it was thoroughly checked (the homework I presumably hadn't done?) *we* would have to wait and see.

Well, I could tell him a thing or two, but he wasn't the only egg in the omelet. The waitress cleared our table and refilled our mugs, coffee here and tea for the lady. The thought of tea at that hour made me shudder, but I could look at the drinker all day.

"So now you know most of it," she said.

"Keeping a stiff upper lip, are we?" Oh, how I love *English* English.

"If anyone is, it's you, and you haven't yet told me why you attended the auction. For all I know, you went there to snatch handbags from dowagers."

"I did, though. My grandfather—"

"Yes *that*, Randal, but I am keen that you held something back. I don't doubt the lonely *–ing*, but there's more, isn't there? You tell, and I'll tell."

Well, heh, a fox *is* known for being crafty. I studied her, and noted that cant of her head when she spoke and it thrilled me as it first had, the night of our impromptu sleeping arrangement, and the way it seemed to accent the shape of her slender nose, a feature that altogether invited challenge, that needed to be engaged, one that would never disappoint if I'd just stick in this mix with her, driven to annoy, in any circumstance bothering her, taking up her time with drivel when I knew she knew: ooh how selfish are such preludes, so I opened up and risked all by revealing my herring-boniest male corset (the only tangible fragment binding past to present as then to now):

"Alright, but bear in mind what I'm going to tell you. I'm over it; I just wanted a memento, some physical item to connect to all the lost time, an epoch spent in treatment, isolated." Boy, was I hedging. She sat, sipping her tea.

"I was an addict, a morpheme addict."

"The *–ing*?"

"Well mostly the *–ing*."

"Now there's irony for you. My uncle has a similar affliction, so I'm a bit familiar with the condition," she said with a wistful smile, but her eyes looked askance at something else and the tension the confession released, like a leaking tire, then re-inflated as ideas gathered air.

"Our meeting wasn't accidental, was it?"

"Oh Randal, come now."

"So much for serendipity."

"We need each other, Randal. Dughall won't stop, he will—"

"Then I shall say to him, recant varlet, thou—"

"Posh! He's off his chump and given to lexical fits!"

I lay back in the booth and regarded her from the oblong; I needed to resize the where of things: softer vowels and crooked tongues checked. If I was hurt, I didn't feel it, so I plunged onward.

"Well, my needs were passive, but the diagnoses were aggressive. They really tried hard to find something else wrong, something deep. I was a disappointment."

"Tell me, Randal, how long were you afflicted?" Her tone suggested I still was, and I recalled faking a relapse twice when the phomorph then treating me was a stunner with Elizabeth Hurley eyes. I'd gotten away with it the first time.

"On and off for a decade, just after grad school; the mid-1990s are a bit of a blur, and I'm still at risk in certain environments; alarms are bad news, rusty bed springs… a gong could be disastrous."

"My uncle is quite the aggressive addict."

"What's his ride?" I asked.

"His what? Speak *English*, will you?"

"His toy."

"I haven't a clue, but I think there must have been many."

"Could it have been an affix? They tend to be popular among British and continental addicts, perhaps due to Latin origins."

"An affix… what are you after?"

"Something he was stuck on, an image reverb or reflexive icon."

"Hmm, now that you mention it, he was such a composite bloody jerk when I worked in his firm, oh! He was what you Yanks call: *an arshole*," she whispered. "I recall a fixation with *all* and words of that ilk. At the time I assumed it was a buzzword, like popular slang; it was a sixties thing, and Mrs. Cline said it went back as far as the war."

"Who was—no, it's okay. You'd encounter a lot of coinage with a bound morpheme such as that one; they're pesky because the ego latches on like a hookworm. See, a free morpheme doesn't require a root, unlike its bound half-twin or, say, the final –ed of your garden variety simple past verb, and they, the free ones I mean, are easy to sling around."

"Well, bully for you, it may well be free but Dughall is enslaved by it."

"How did he get it?"

For an answer she slid out of the booth and headed for the door. I paid the check and caught up to her and we trotted along, her heels tapping time like a snare drum.

I said, now what's wrong, and the whole front row of fatties erupted as Chamois tapped his foot while measuring his response. But I was beginning to grow weary; his interlocutions were more pedantic than didactic and I'd noticed a nagging discomfort, an abrasive lump that I couldn't shift. He seemed to have lost sight of his opening dictum; I would err because I was supposed to, and that being especially true with women given their independent nature and sinuous unpredictability. Where did he get these ideas?

"You want to tell me where we're headed?" We'd walked four blocks and she hadn't spoken, though her body English said *Watch Out*: the tapping toe as we stopped at crosswalks and the arms locked firmly beneath her pointers. It was good exercise after our meal, so I just tagged apace, right on up the steps of the public library.

"Is chivalry dead?" she said, before the massive bronze and glass doors.

"Yes! It was slain by sexism."

"Oh, that is rot. Open the door, Randal." Quasimodo obeyed and in we went, but there the charade ended as I snagged a magazine and sat. Thirty minutes later she took the chair next to mine and crossed a killer leg, but I pretended not to notice.

"You'll be pleased to know I have made a discovery," she said.

I stared at the magazine, suddenly unable to recall the article I'd been reading.

"It's about my uncle," she said.

I turned a page. We sat like that a while in the murmur and rustle that is the very breath of a library; its only permissible language as the repository of our greatest words.

"What is so bloody fascinating about trucks?" she said at last. The two-page Chevy ad loomed before me and I felt, well, like a rock.

"You're miffed, aren't you," she said with a merry lilt.

"I don't do doors, your *majesty*."

"Oh bollocks, you never know where a door may lead," she said, crossing the other leg, the skirt riding higher as she swung her foot, making sure that I saw. But it's a game that men (shut up Chamois!) are ill prepared to play well after losing round one, maybe because victory is as intangible as the rules, so I dodged the parry.

"Claudia, first the rest of the story: give me all of it. Do that for me and then I'll listen to your discovery." She continued the leg swing as she appraised me, smiling with her eyes.

"Alright, and you will see how they entwine. Lincoln's excised morpheme, *all*, was indeed presented to P.M. Roget. I recall a tintype in the attic, a mise en scene of the dignified gathered under Union Jack bunting. To my knowledge he never put it to use, but it was handed down from one generation to the next, until one day it vanished, but my uncle Dughall believes it to be in my possession, and he's rather a nut." A matronly clerk approached and asked us to keep our voices down, which was a hoot. I guess too much whispering is a desecration of the sanctity of pseudo silence, and I thought I could outline a story about a librarian who signs up for a course in yelling. Meanwhile, Claudia had been going on, so here's the gist of it.

Upon graduation she'd gone to work as an editor in her uncle's public relations firm, but didn't remain long after her initiation into office politics, namely the Sapphic attentions of her immediate boss, a cunning linguist, and her uncle's petty schemes to pry from her the locale of her birthright morpheme, about which his obsession became all too apparent; it was during this time that she observed him, *spied* would be more accurate, twitching in conniptional fits of logorrhea (a condition I well knew) and concluded he was mad, so she resigned and soon after departed for New York and a new haven.

"All right, thank you," I said. "Now, what did you uncover?"

"He is here in this city." I didn't question how she'd found out, for any reference librarian worth their reading speed would have found it in moments, the response I expected to get for a book I needed.

"Here," she handed over a printout. It showed the name of an ad agency uptown, but the date on the sheet was eight years old.

"Did you cross check the phone book?"

"Well of course. They are not listed, but it is plain as a pikestaff he is here."

"Any ad agency with more than a whiteboard is going to be listed," I said.

She pouted as I went off to get my book. I also double checked her query, a fruitless errand.

We spent the rest of that day cleaning up her apartment and dealing with the mess of havoc's train, police, landlord, building manager, as well as Claudia's calm which I took for reserved British anger. I suggested she stay with me for the time being and her relief, though mixed with ire, was palpable.

"Okay, let's hit the trail," I said, hefting two suitcases.

"You Yanks and your frontier language: how can anyone lionize such a horrific as a time when men were men and sheep were scared?"

I wasn't going to be baited. "I stand apart. There's not a fringe of buckskin in my armoire, dear."

"You haven't an armoire," she said.

"Or anything else, but you see what I mean. Besides, there hasn't been a wagon train lately; we ran out of Westward Ho!"

"You're all cowboys at heart anyway," she said, and flagged a taxi.

"You'll never see a ten-gallon hat on this buckaroo. If I wanted to look ridiculous, I'd find a better way." That got a laugh, and it was nice to break her mood. As we rode across town, I noted how on the downside of a weekend Sunday afternoon faces already looked dour, as though prepping for the morning. Then she was back at it.

"But it's not clothing or idiomatic speech; it's that frontier attitude common to Americans. Didn't you suggest we put up a tent in Central Park?"

"The great outdoors!"

"I rest my case."

"Listen, I've done some hiking and camping, although I'm no John Muir. But check this out: there are guys who can tell the time of day by looking at the sun.

Me, I've never been able to make out the numbers," (a line lifted from bug-bomb-bank-robber Harvey Welch; who better to steal from than a thief?) and that got her giggling, and Chamois started in too, but I couldn't be sure if he was laughing with me or at me, so I just pasted on a grin and sat there like a dunce.

"I know what you mean," she said. "I always wondered what good it would do to locate the North Star if you were lost. You're not about to stalk off when you can't see a thing, and in the morning, it's gone."

"Well, all we need here is a good cabby, or GPS." The driver agreed with the first part and sped off into traffic and got us back to my apartment where soon after we ordered takeout, and with chopsticks in hand I reached for the library book that I hoped would enlighten me as to how to get a handle on a new patient, an egregious exaggerator, as I had misplaced the tome reserved for such cases. While reviewing the jacket notes, the phone rang.

"Mr. Poe, this is Detective Kearns, NYPD, I'd like to ask you several questions."

"I believe I told you and a number of officers all I know, here and at the station."

"Then I'd say a recap of it will be a breeze, am I right?" I went through the whole thing again, but I left out the romantic interlude.

"This Claudia Roget, how long had you known her before the break in?"

"We had just met, as I mentioned a moment ago, and earlier."

"Yes, that's right, just met. The funny thing is that her apartment and yours were tossed by the same person or people, same day, same MO, same footprint if you get my meaning."

"No, detective Kearns, I'm not sure that I do."

"Do you have enemies Poe, anyone who would wish you harm?"

"Enemies? Well, no; in fact, it's almost laughable."

"The NYPD isn't laughing Mr. Poe."

I thought then of several clients who'd accused me of shaping or misshaping their addiction to include a host of morphemes which seemingly were unimaginable prior to my counseling sessions, yet both were admen, former copywriters enslaved by the rhythm of award-winning jingles. But the violent manner in which my place—our places had been ransacked didn't seem to fit either of them; it was too wild a conjecture.

"Well, let me bring you up to speed," said the detective, "Ms. Roget's place was tossed prior to yours, which means that we had come and interviewed her long before you discovered a similar mess at your apartment, but Ms. Roget gave your number as an emergency contact some ten hours before you say the two of you first met. Can you explain that?" There must have been a mistake somewhere in the reporting and I said as much but he just rambled on with his angle that there was something that perhaps I hadn't told him, and indeed there was; that my meeting with Claudia had been scripted; that somehow, she knew I would be there; that we would need each other and very soon; that I would fall in love with her? The last was so presumptuous that it tended to unravel all the other tentacles and leave me flabbered and just plain gasted, too. I was supposed to be upset that a witty and articulate and engagingly sexy woman had set a trap to seduce me? What would Freud have done? Gone out and bought a pack of rubbers.

I returned to the book's jacket and began to read about the new client.

5

In this seminal work, one that launched a brilliant academic career yet may have ended it as well, Professor Norse Charlton, Ph.D. Llewellyn College, Cambridge, presents a lively argument for the origins of hyperbole in ancient texts as a backdrop to its explosive impact on English Renaissance tropes within the dynamic of his thesis: a revelation of Sprites dabbling in human affairs to shape the course of literary history!

However, that same blurb writer had this to say in the preface:

Nothing short of balderdash and flummery herein, with resources based on supposition and hearsay, this nonetheless well-written expose attempts with scholarly erudition to hoodwink us all with citations from apocryphal Druids to the outright imaginations of children.

From the inside flap I learned more about the author and that the current text was a reprint that included the critical commentary generated by the first edition, much of it in the pejorative, for it had been published at a time prior to the sensationalism of science as entertainment through the writers the like of Carl Sagan or Stephen Hawking.

I was intrigued on several accounts. First, there was my own scholarly study of tropes, the dry, often pedantic exposition of facts and sources that one plows through in graduate study, the furrows of the thesis garden, whereas this book looked like fun. Secondly, there was my patient, Dr. Wallis Fordham, a recidivist morpheme addict on the one hand but a Renaissance scholar on the other, and it seemed likely that this book and its author would be a good opening gambit at our next consultation. I dabbled in the opening chapter that dealt with the ancient Greeks but soon skimmed ahead to the Renaissance only to find myself essentially where I had begun, subsequent to a footnote that the dialog was obtained from secondary sources:

'By far the most famous of the arguments of Oberon and Titania is that which erupted over the changeling Indian boy that Oberon wanted for his own and that Titania determined to keep, no matter what, as tempests raged and the seasons trembled and Robin Goodfellow was sent upon his merry deed. But there were in abundance other arguments just as heady and from confidential sources deep in the Hedge Wood have I this to share:

'It is clear that our influence in the human world wanes and we see forward what becomes of it, so we must not dally further but rekindle the human hope in good and trust in goodliness that comes apace. What say ye, wife?'

'Yea, though I mentioned this very thing not a fortnight ago, do you not recall?'

'No. What I do recall is your hiding of the changeling, Hyperbole, once again beneath your skirts; he is old and wise enough now to fend, I believe,' said Oberon.

'*She*, you bag of wax, and she fends well for me and ever shall.'

'Our needs are not of import here, woman, we must rescue those whose indifference will bring us to harm, and you know this as well as I.'

'Perchance, why this one when so many sprites will carry the banner, will lay down their lives for the sake of this realm?'

'Aye, the reason dear wife is intrinsic to the success we will achieve, for the changeling is both a he and a she, as well as human and fay; we have none other quite so talented, quite so wily, so swift among the moon shrouds and sure upon the earth.'

'Well ahead of you then again am I, dear husband, for I choose Hyperbole to go among the humans and turn their heads.'

'You? Why I just spoke of it!'

'Tell me how you see her uplifting the aura of our realm, now that we agree.'

'Wife, you tempt the hairs on my head to rise and shroud cocoon about you!' {They embraced then and Oberon laid open his plan}

'The writers of this age and that coming are conducting works that do little to enliven us. They do not engage the winkle but rather the weight and it is of iron; they little possess wisdom enough to complete one scroll before emboweling themselves on the phallus of fame, no this is not the way, and as we see faerie influence has waned since proud Hellas when musai went among them to spread grandiloquence. I chuckle to recall my friend Dionysus sending maenads and satyrs to exalt Aristophanes and embrace the tenor of agon and episode, strophe and antistrophe with lofty exaggeration, and so shall I send among them not legions this time but a single and powerful sprite to enliven the artisans with a resonance that will expand with magnitude the further he goes—'

'She!'

'Alright then, I shall kiss the thunder clouds the day I say again *he*—and the further she goes the greater the deed and the broader the audience to charm with the beauty of the faerie realm, for she will be one too powerful to fall by the wayside of human lusts.'

'She goes so far that I lose sight of the day I will again see her face. Husband, do this for me, for us: send after her another to match her stride and wipe her brow, one who may also report from one eon to the next, for I shall catch my breath for word of her doing.'

'So shall it be. Along with Hyperbole we will send Kairos for her gender and her shape will shift with the seasons and adapt with the changing of the times, to archive and to chronicle, and should either lose their way the other may guide them through the whorls of Time.'

Perusing the critical essays in the appendices, I discovered that quite appropriately this initial chapter had been the departure point for many. One essay was devoted entirely to a debunking of the fabled Hedge Wood in the Egerian Forest that Charlton had claimed once stood in Northumbria, and it went so far as to buttonhole soil scientists with carbon samples from petrified wood that might have originated anywhere, and that got me to drifting and I thought of the Lady of the Lake who, offering up a sword, mutated into rhythmic verses of Alfred Tennyson himself rolling me into the ages, rocking me as though in a cradle, but then I opened my eyes and saw it was all of them in the form of Claudia, staring into me as though she saw beyond my dozing slumber and read the images scrolled on my eyes; I held out my hands and she drew me up from the chair and led me off to bed.

6

The next morning, we went off to work with the teeming millions. It had been quite a weekend: I had blundered into a poodle, a romance, and a mystery, with the presumed villain behind the caper none other than a type of person whose phonemic footprint I thoroughly understood because I had been there myself; I could read him like a stutter. The absence of eye contact in the subway allowed me to sense a likeness of him, brooding nearby, pale in the jaundice of utterance as the train thundered uptown. Then it was up the staircase and into the jabbering streets where I hiked the usual three blocks to the office. When I turned the corner, I thought for a moment the annual street fair had jumped the gun until I recognized Melody lingering at the edge of a throng. I walked over and said, what's up?

"Doc, help him if you can."

"You're a doctor? Help him, help him," sang a swarthy tradesman, along with others.

"Mel here is a doctor, too," I stated, as they tugged me to where a corpulent jogger lay sprawled on the sidewalk, green in the gills, blue in the face, and white lipped; it was clear he was choking. I stood there like a dunce, but then knelt by him and caught retching gasps of consonant clusters, and instinct took over:

"Listen quickly! Think vowels: A, E, I, O, U, focus on vowels and vowels only." The rasp continued unabated but his golf ball eyes undilated and before long the hack lost its laborious *ck-ck* until the rest of it wheezed out, flapping like the sound of cards being shuffled around whatever he'd swallowed. Paramedics arrived then, waved me aside, and bent over the man. I was as stunned as anyone bystanding there when they tweezered from his gullet a pink plastic shopping bag, our all too urban and ubiquitous airborne scourge of capitalism's worst take on modernism: billowing over alleys and thruways, aloft in aerial stunts between the ballet of cars; it's Andy Warhol's *Trash* mutated a billionfold, swirling and settling ever into drainage to make their way like sci-fi salmon down from the hill to the sea; your garden variety dolphin killer. As the paramedics set up the gurney, I stood, felt the blood drain from my head as Melody's face blurred and I reached out to her. When I next looked around, I didn't know where I was, and four of the five question words were pulling my puppet strings.

"He's coming around," said a voice to my left, and it issued from a man standing next to Melody, a doctor.

"Oh Randal, you're back! I was so worried, but you're okay!"

"Where did I go," I said, grasping that I lay in a hospital bed. They smiled, the two, fawning.

"The last thing I recall, I was telling the EMT about vowels, and he didn't believe me."

"You had what's commonly known as a heat stroke," said the doctor. He took my hand in both of his: "Doctor Alden Lyfe, I am most pleased to make your acquaintance Dr. Poe. Thanks to you, pigs didn't kill that man. He was lucky you were there, and in turn I feel lucky that they brought you here."

"Pigs, in the city?"

"Look, with all the plastic now, some number in the quadtrillions, it was only a matter of time."

"I don't get it." I looked over at Melody.

"Plastic Invasive Gag Syndrome; we see it all the time now. Happens mostly to joggers but even children are at risk; there's just too much of the stuff floating around out there. But from what your colleague here has told me, we may be on the brink of a great medical breakthrough with what you did today." He held my wrist again and nodded.

"I passed out, is that it?"

"Not before you gave him vowels."

"The EMT called me a smartass, and that's the last I remember." I flashed on the similarity between this schism and the dreams I'd been having lately, awakening from each of them with a sense that time had removed a chapter while I was gone, but that I was somehow part of that missing text.

"Well, put yourself in his shoes," said Melody. "To us it makes perfect sense, but to that EMT, well, he thought you were sassing him, until you keeled over."

"Well, I couldn't have made it any plainer: gagging is glottal consonant constriction; I calmed the guy down and got him breathing *through* the plastic, as it were." Melody gave me a hug and then left for the office and damage control. The doctor sat on the opposite bed while I got dressed.

"We could make a mint, an absolute fortune on this if we played it right," he said.

"A mint."

"Look at it; it's the perfect combination, a phono-morphologist and a medical doctor. See, your profession gives it authenticity, mine, validity. For marketing I know an outfit," he said.

"Look, Dr. Lyfe, I may no longer appear woozy, but I might as well be."

"We put vowels in a can—no, an aerosol tube, like pepper spray, except here, you've got a cure-all for PIGS! Think of it, how many people would keep a tube of it in their pocket, handbag, and glove-box? Millions, and that's what we'd stand to make, you and I, what do you say?"

"I say you're in need of some quality time off. Look, for one thing it is utterly unethical, not to mention downright dishonest," I said, noting the alliteration and wondering if I was coming down with something.

"Not ethical? Why, that's ridiculous. Look, a good twenty percent of any treatment is the patient's will to be cured, to be whole again, that great galloping urge to again be neck and neck in the race."

"You cannot put vowels in a can."

"Well, of course not," he grinned, "but look, we'll put a disclaimer on the bottom or a ring of microscopic font along the side; this could be the greatest panacea ever."

"Or the greatest lawsuit," I said, and reached for my shoes.

"By the way, where am I?"

"Cedars of Palestine Hospital," he said. "But before you go, just a little background on what we're looking at here: we had a field day; it was cash and carry all the way; this is going back a dozen years, because no HMO would touch it. But it wasn't going to last forever. First, a pre-existing condition ended the free-for-all, and then the whole system overhaul scotched it for good, that is, until today. Think this through with me, we could revive PIGS as a cash cow and never look back."

"What was the pre-existing condition," I asked, fully aware of their prevalence in my own field, not as an insurance issue, but rather one of morphophonological origin.

"Birth."

"Birth?"

"It was then, and most likely remains, the greatest preemptive catch on record, and let me tell you, the cash basis made it approachable, but even then, it was a tough bastard for treatment; nobody really knew what to do; it wasn't on the books anywhere. What we had was battalions of beached dolphin, squadrons of seabirds and fish by the shipload, all with plastic tangled gullets; but nobody was putting it together. The first umpteen zillion cases were a windfall and not only because we charged out the wazoo—our patients lived! But that said, no two treatments were the same; we ran the gamut from mouth-to-mouth to the Jaws of Life. If someone had said *vowels* back then we'd have thrown him on a gurney and removed his gall bladder."

"So, hypothetically, we're just putting air in a can and claiming it will save a life?"

"Oh no, we won't make any claims at all other than for what happened today in the style of an info-mercial, then we say: 'as seen on TV'; believe me, it'll work, we make back our investment ten, twenty-fold, even more." I was dressed and ready to go.

"Well Doctor Lyfe, it's been interesting. I will consider this request and get back to you." We shook hands, and in a Bronx two minutes I was in a cab.

Why had I hedged at the end, not telling him what I thought about gimmickry? The tintinnabulation of a distant nerve struck would resound louder given time.

Instead, I reviewed what I knew about the Cedars, primarily because of their psyche ward, and I wondered if that was where Lyfe spent his days. But the ride uptown got me thinking of other pigs, and I wondered if Bessboro was ever so afflicted. What would the Honeycutts do if their stock began choking on plastic: pigs with PIGS! Then the acronym got me to thinking on my days as an intern after a decade in journalism.

7

Following onward from my own treatment for morpheme addiction, and while I trained in phono-morphology, I had taken up a counseling position because they were short- handed, and sat on the other side of the desk. It seemed I had the knack, and so they let me stay on, and it was there at the Linguist-aholic Improvement Proprietary Services, Inc. that I put myself through graduate school. LIPS Inc was then the premier clinic of its kind in North America. We received funding from a host of far-ranging donors among who were the Modern Association of Phono-morphologists (MAP), the Clever Hans Anecdotal Society, Manhattan chapter (CHASM), and Mensa Outreach for Jargon Orthography (MOJO), all of which helped to pay for the treatment of phonology freaks known as A-As or Articulation Addicts {a.k.a. Vox Popinjays for the worst of their supercilious lot}, Syntax Sinners, who more often than not were failed poets, Allomorph Addicts or A-A-2s, whose adherence to neologisms render their utterances incomprehensible, and even Mummers stuck in rhyming couplets, where records indicate more often than not the role of the Quack Doctor. Just then, one of them loomed over me.

"Mr. Poe, an overuse of the acronym is the beginning writer's way of hiding from the obvious, much the way a faux artist palms a palette of flashy pastels in garish panoply," said Chamois. Even as the tubs tittered, I knew he had me, and I would have stridden from the room then and there if it hadn't been for his own addictive allegiance to alliteration: an odious obeisance to an onerous obbligato. But I needed to tell it the way it needed to be told, I told him, that it almost seemed to be writing itself, willing itself onto the page as though I were a mere bystander, a lackey holding the pen tray, dusting the ink well.

That changed his tone, and upon dismissing the others he pulled up a chair. Tell me more, he said.

"Well, as a certified phono-morphologist I can assure you that the people we treat are in every way ordinary, so you can wipe that leer off your face. While we do get many professors, psychologists, and high-caliber thinkers, they all began their lives as did you and I. Now, current theory holds that verbs or verb phrases are the catch points, the brambles that catch in your clothing as you traverse the fields of language. However, deconstructionists posit that—

"Now there's an odd bunch for you," said Chamois, "they tend to make for lousy fiction writers. Beyond that, I don't really understand the theory."

"Well, it has to do with binary opposites, but don't worry; there's no one outside of a college philosophy department that understands it either. Anyway, they posit that initial morphemes, more commonly known as *baby talk*, are the culprits and whether syllables, words, or mix-word hybrids (my own first utterance: *noosbylont*) they enrapture their victim but then become dormant, lying doggo for years until they are tripped by some magneto as yet not understood. By then, they roost deep within the psyche and help to form the hearth and home of who you are and not even a top-shelf Jungian Svengali could fork them out. Whichever theory one chooses as the fulcrum, nouns and noun phrases do seem to follow those of the verb families and thus takes one step further Noam Chomsky and others' belief that language is inherent; you're born with a prewired distributor in the engine of your ability to know how languages work."

"Nice metaphor," said Chamois.

"Thank you."

"I have a better understanding now," he said.

"We're not quite finished: morpheme addiction is the linguistic equivalent of Tourette's syndrome and is marked by uncontrollable vocalic tics; orgasmic spasms of consonant clusters and white-water vowel streams hurtling among the bound and free morphemes of English, a turbulent caterwaul of the oral."

"Might I add: the opiate of onomatopoeia?" he suggested.

"Not at all. Why, to a morpheme junky, onomatopoeia is a cheap high; it is the lexical equivalent of Tokay or Scuppernong."

Chamois and I parted when I noted the pile of mail I had just opened, the opener in my hand, the office. Then the phone rang.

"Yes, this is Doctor Poe."

"My appointment today was handled by a clown."

"And which circus was that," I said. If he wasn't going to identify himself, the opening gambit of communicative interaction, I saw no need to play the straight man.

"Why, Barnum and Bailey: The Greatest Show on Earth."

"As a kid, I went there a half dozen times," I said.

"I went there a million times."

"You and the midget in the cannon, or perhaps you are him?"

"I had elephants for breakfast every day." I toyed with how much wadding it'd take for each lanyard pull of the midget shot; the receiving end of crank calls can make for fun, if you're holding your mouth right.

"Pachyderms packed with Picante and peppers are wonderful, I'm told," said the caller, "but lions are better; I had twenty a day for snacks."

"Not too prideful, are you?"

"That's about as funny as a screen door on a submarine," he said.

"I had a sinking feeling you would say that."

"I am not coming today," he said.

"Neither am I; today I am going, that's Mister Going to you, but perhaps tomorrow I'll be Coming." I was growing weary of not knowing to whom I was serving in a ping-pong of symbiotic flapdoodle. Melody came in just then, and I told the caller I had to go.

"Alright, I'll sue for peace and come in. What are your terms?"

"A name, give me a name. Okay, Mr. Charlton, we'll see you at three." Charlton. I guessed it wasn't the author. No sober academic would act like a child.

"Well, I've had every three"— I hung up and wandered into her office.

"How do you feel?"

"I'm fine, really."

"The guy was out jogging," she said, "and he just sucked it in; I can't get over it."

"You know, I remember when I used to walk home from school, I was like six, seven, and I'd look for discarded bottles, Coke, Nehi, Sprite amid the more general plastic trash. I went past this construction site, or maybe more than just one; there were always bottles that had been chucked out in the grass beside the road. I used to look up at the sky through the bottle glass, turning the bottle to make a ripple effect and Coke's ribbed light green bottle was the best," I said.

She looked at me for a while before speaking. "Every now and then these choice fragments of the younger you come through the ether and they're always colorful but seldom referential," she said.

"Well then, allow me to enlighten you. What we witnessed today first hand, from front row seats, is how thoroughly awful we've been to our planet in what, fifty-some years. We've gone from soda bottles tossed where kids can collect 'em to what we saw today. There was nothing like that then; sure, there was trash, but it didn't sail through the air, and you think about it, they're everywhere now, and we've become so inured we never think about it, our frame of reference is so skewed we don't blink an eye, we stand there like that crowd and watch a man choke to death." She came around her desk and began to massage my neck and shoulders.

"Randal, he didn't die thanks to you, and I think they wanted to help but had no training in CPR or whatever, and they were scared. But your point is a valid one; there *were* no bags or other plastic floating or flying about anywhere. You know I grew up on boats. People didn't jettison shopping bags or anything else. Gig Harbor was a clean town, still is, but, you know, let's put this behind us by bringing it forward, as you so often say."

"I'll tell you what, you Google it while I go and meditate. I need to unwind, relax, and go silently ape shit." And that's just what I did. Then like a zombie I went to the three o'clock relaxed enough to expose a fraud, or at the least one whose addiction was sought but never caught, a wannabe. His exaggerations were clever but contrived, and he at last admitted as much; he was only trying to spice up the humdrum, pump a little color into the pallor of the day-to-day: viz, the phone call. Yet he had other issues that I exposed quite by accident when I said I had read his book and suggested he exaggerate something worthwhile, like the Great Vowel Shift, as to when it happened and so forth. He took the bait and maintained that the vowel shift was ongoing, but he repeatedly got snagged in double-yews, often stringing them together alliteratively in a manner that wasn't forced, and so uncovered a predilection for voiced bilabial nasals and glides, as he said:

"*When* is known and of little interest, so forget the *when*, and look to *what* and *why* and *wonders will well* up around you. Why, for example, did long vowels become short, stressed become unstressed and so on, is one of the great rhetorical questions of the age, weighed in willy-nilly by wistful theoreticians, the push and the pull, the yin and the yang, but if you ask me I would say the so-called shift, if ever there was one, had been building for some time and was wistfully winnowed from the forest, and I do not mean the forest of dialects of which Midland grew the tallest stands of timber, nay t'was the Egerian Forest from which the dialectical shift emerged like a storm, a whirling wind of wattles, and brought trailing along soon after, like the train of Tatiana's gown, a new lexicon, a wondrous, wending word-hoard." As he paused, staring off into the centuries, I recalled similar passages from his book and that this was the area that had gotten him in trouble. Whether one took a side at all (and most would not), the history of English linguistics was heady stuff; I looked over my notes and egged him on:

"Doctor Charlton, are you referring to inkhorn words?"

"A scurrilous term."

"How so, if I may?"

"The multitude of means by which our English vocabulary expanded during the Early Modern period is well known," he said.

"Such as the increase in literacy levels, if I recall?"

"That, and from Caxton making readily available to just about anyone at all the classical texts, the Bible foremost among them, and as well from the Protestant Reformation; their translations borrowed heavily from Latin and Greek, yet these recognized trends were but a masque to the marvelous, a windfall of well-being for all: a spirited intervention in mortal affairs; it had been planned for some time."

"Wasn't there opposition to the heavy borrowing of terminology?"

"By whom—oh, you mean mortals, our silly ancestors; they couldn't have stopped the flow with an army; there were some ten thousand new words during the Renaissance alone."

"I'm afraid that you've lost me… the spirited intervention, let's go back to that."

"A measure of their majestic munificence, it was."

He stared, perhaps deciding whether I stood with or against him, and to help him out in that regard, I delved into the bilabial fixation, convinced that it was *voice* at the root of his jones; his tone had been pejorative, talking down to me but his facial expressions denoted uncertainty, even disbelief. Though he had yet to exaggerate as he had on the phone, I went out on a limb to posit that here sat a man whose literal voice (in academia) had been truncated, reduced to a whine and that the only voice left to him from which he might salvage some dignity had been his larynx, and from there he rode forth to tilt at windmills larger than life. As most do, he laughed at the folly of holding a scrap of paper before his maw as he varied voiced and voiceless sounds. I slid a booklet of limericks across the desk for him to practice with.

"Now, I would say we have concluded here and you need not come back, although you may at any time, if only to chat over coffee. But, tell me if you would, and this is off the clock, the spirits you mentioned before, and their mortal imposition. I'm intrigued, you see; I have read your book, *The Legend of Hyperbole,* and I found it fascinating."

He smiled. "You seem a rather bright sort of fellow, history interest you?"

"Well, as an undergrad, I double-majored: English and Journalism, minor in History, and I've never really stopped reading across those disciplines."

"Tell me." He scooted the chair closer to the desk and smiled, "your most ardent query in all of that magic. Something that left you dissatisfied."

"Well, since we're headed there, we were rushed through Piers Ploughman, I believe, to make way for the Faerie Queen; while not denigrating the latter, Piers was too swift to salute."

"Yes, interesting, but did the Red Kross knight leave anything unsolved for you?"

"I had a blast unpacking that stuff. What a great poem. And another, I was really taken with Le Mort D' Arthur, if there was anything that, you know, would resonate, I think it would be Merlin's end; it seems he didn't deserve it." His smile had remained fixed, his eyeballs, drilling into mine.

"Didn't he now."

"Well, you have to look at—let me rephrase, you have to keep it in the story frame forever as a parallel. If you remove it and cast about in script-writing fashion, for example, you end up with the poor sorcerer an early victim of deforestation, but history as his story not over yet—"

"Unable to free himself—"

"Maybe ends up in the mast of a frigate, could be either English or French, and goes down in the Channel or who knows."

"And kept within the frame, what then?"

"Well, if you ask me, he's still there, by now in petrified or protected wood, maybe wetlands, and only your *spirited intervention* would free him; angels not of the stylized kind, depraved by culture. You spoke a moment ago about an otherworld connection."

"Yes, to be blunt, our friend Merlin would have been trapped for five hundred years when a team of sprites sallied forth to improve our communicative competence, and to increase our interaction with our language, their language to be quite frank, and no pun intended, and in so doing expand our involvement with them and make favorable the otherworld, to slow its declination by enlivening rhetoric—simply sprinkling dust on artisans wasn't working anymore, or less effectively due to metals ever on the increase, traces, yokes, rowels, bits and buckles and the like; there had always been swords but now plowshares too! So, words, new words of glorious and demulcent charge were brought forth, and it was their emergence that truly sparked the aforementioned influences, and all together they changed the course of language, and of history, and still do. I have angered many a scholar when I suggest that the lexicon introduced by Erasmus hadn't been wholly his own and that, *On Copia of Words and Ideas*, the Strunk and White of the Middle Ages, owed a debt of gratitude to *Egregia*, and should have cited her. Now, as to your mention of inkhorn, I apologize for the cranky remark," he said.

"Not at all."

"My association with that term differs radically from that of my contemporaries, you understand. For it is well known that some of the lexemes introduced didn't 'make it' and we no longer have them today, they are *exolete*, to name one. Why did some words prosper and others languish? No one ever seemed able to provide an answer; well, I have! The same sprites that brought them exiled them, and over time this removal, this taking away became, for those faeries, what we might think of as an obsessive-compulsive disorder, or one, rather, its partner a companion of sorts, divided from the original like an amoeba. Yet, a negating process employed hand-by-hand against, a third, it isn't clear, has ever been in pursuit, tidying up. Lexemes may not be removed completely even if their usage is defunct, for they are elementals in the continuum. From reading my book you're aware that I suggest our current state of affairs is the result of many words removed as late as the 18th century. But I don't stop there; I posit that certain thematic lexemes trigger like events down the halls of time and that I can determine what words are missing based upon what wrinkles, as I call them, have, well, wrinkled. I have been roundly hooted by forensic linguists, but I stand firm."

I was well acquainted with some forms of the collegiate derision of which he spoke, for legions of linguists and speech pathologists had openly ridiculed and railed against phono-morphology as a field, some still do.

"Now, you may well be wondering how I could criticize the like of old Desiderius Erasmus for poor scholarship while not going on to name the sources on which I have relied heavily, perhaps too heavily, for my reputation in academia seems to be somewhat in tatters.

Oddly, I have become a sort of underground champion of wiccans and warlocks and all manner of new age spiritist ilk. In fact, I have a speaking engagement, part of a lecture series, all this week. Would you care to attend, Dr. Poe?"

8

When we parted at the elevator, I realized how tired I was and knew it was unlikely I'd attend his lecture. It was Miller Time. As I was readying to depart, Claudia called to say she had received crank calls at work that day, and that she was frightened of going home to her apartment. Would I care to accompany her? I thought we'd agreed she would stay with me, but I let it slide; would a fox ignore a hen house? I suggested we meet at a bar I frequented, near my place in Midtown. It was drizzling when she showed up in a damp pantsuit, and we kissed.

"Hey, sweet, how'd you get so wet?"

"If you must know, I walked quite a way here."

"Whatever for, aren't there enough taxis uptown?"

"He was following me."

"Who—wait a second, let's back up. You walked a zillion blocks because someone was following you?"

"No, silly, I went to look at a broach I saw at Cartier and caught him peeping, plain as a pikestaff," she said, digging around in her bag. I ordered a martini and Stout for myself and drank some before pushing on.

"Well, guys are always checking you out, sweet. That's probably drool on you."

"You would think of that, Randal," she said, tilting a compact at coiffure.

"All the more reason for us to be together, chivalry will rise from the ashes like a pouter pigeon phoenix."

"What? Listen to me, darling. He was following me so I hailed a taxi. By then, I was quite soaked through."

"Well, let's get you home and out of those wet duds."

"But he'll be wetter, won't he?" Across the street a hatless man stood under a hat shop awning as though posing for an agency ad. Could this cardboard character really be somebody?

"C'mon," I said, dropping money on the table and grabbing her hand, but not before she gulped her drink, and we headed for the door. Traffic was against us and the guy took advantage of it and was in a cab before we crossed. Claudia waved down another one while I kept my eyes on the departing cab. "Follow that taxi!" I nearly cried, fulfilling a dream, perchance to yell, but it slurped out as verbal drainage in caterwaul: "Tax*ing*! Tax*ing*! Tax*ing*! Tax*ing*! Tax*ing*!"

"Wheech toxi mon?" With Claudia's grip depending my jaws, I slowed to a whirl of woofs and grunts and got control of the shakes and jitters. But there was no time for pleasantries as the driver piloted through a George Raft scene that I knew Chamois would deplore:

"What you have to understand is that it's been done a million times."

"But everything in New York's been done a million times," I hedged.

"And that is precisely why it fails to excite, don't you see? Almost every contrivance of escape and of the chase has been gleaned and laid bare, almost every angle has been covered," he said, crossing his legs. He seemed so much less the tyrant seated in one of the chairs vacated by the davenport tubs.

"Wait, are you suggesting that by *almost* there's still something unfound?"

"Perhaps there is, but it's up to you to find it. And to do that you need a solid grounding in the bases of fiction. Without a foundation, you'll fail to locate that crevice in the attic."

"That crevice that holds the gold half-button sliced from your grandfather's tunic by the assassin with the lancet, and to which the inheritance is held by a scarlet thread?"

"Poe, sometimes you amaze me. In the ebb of your smartass lurks a fine imagination. Stop fighting me, and I'll be of some help to you," he said, rising. He gathered his satchel and his smokes and bid me adieu.

We trailed the taxi to a brownstone on West 48th Street where the cheap-ass raincoat ascended the steps to a door that struck me as one majestic enough to admit a Nero Wolfe, but it sure was odd. I'd only been in this hood twice, once to accompany home a dazed professor who'd departed a session quoting Macbeth backwards, and the second, when a buddy turned up with an Asian family in tow and tales of teaching English abroad, and we'd scoured these neighborhoods for promising flats. Now, we sat in a taxi with the clicking meter marching against us and that closed door gave us nothing. I tapped the driver and off we went. But where did we go? I time-traveled back to the days when I sat on the other side of the desk as a morpheme addict and knew then and there that my outburst had lain doggo in the brain pan for years only to erupt in a moment of excited panic; I didn't see how I could be of help to Claudia at all if indeed I was losing my grip.

"So, I'm at a drawbridge," I said.

"Hah!" Chamois paused and laughed again. "Dear boy, I believe you have hit a wall, as we say. But only our dear friend Pancho can front a drawbridge and gain our arousal. Haha! Yes, thank you for the image. How may I help?" The taxi dropped us at my place and feeling a sudden loss of appetite, I took to my bed.

Turning toward the faint glow in the east I saw etched against the purple a horizon lined with books until they faded upward into black; then turning to the left with the spreading gray into rosy pink I knew too that behind me as well, the four corners were made of books, a library of the soul that expanded with breath, its own respiration trembling mine. We were in a room that resembled the class room except for that it was outside as well as inside, a mirror of a mirror, and Chamois loomed, perched on a stool that went up to the rafters and was as high as the shelves all lined with books that went on up to crepuscular cornices but he swiveled his stool to leer and his grin ballooned in my face and the sentences all began with adjectives. Sentences that wound around the stacks, spiraling upward, dizzy following them I fell time and again, to be admonished again and start anew. To sleep, perchance to read, but soon I was entwined and the sentences ran like vines to my neck and wrapped about tightly so I sat up in bed and spat, phatooowee, and the shattered dream dissolved to sparkling dust that assumed the form of a winged fairy that flitted in and out before it arced over the foot board and caromed off the metal trash can lid I stole from Greenpeace before they went plastic.

Awake, I pushed myself up to lean against the headboard, ruminating, touched by the departing images but clinging to them with that sudden flash that I had been there, that instant snapshot of familiarity where in a single heartbeat you know the location—and then it passed. Claudia entered and stretched out beside me.

"Good morning, Sweet." She glommed one and laughed. This was a good morning for sure; she looked great. How do they do that, first thing, with the sun!

"You know, I had the strangest dream," I said.

"About me," she said, around her tongue in my ear, and I turned into her and we rolled and arranged the measures of ourselves.

"Now, tell me your dream and without Chamois butting in every topic sentence." What did she know, but I was too waxed lying crossways in scissored legs, staring up at the little swirled nip of her bellybutton and the curve of the bird's nest and the upward sweep of ribcage to those luscious—books?

"It was a library or like a library somewhere out on the edge of time. I don't know how I know that I just do, you know. Our friend Chamois was the librarian or he's a guardian for the place and there were millions of books, no, not millions but the sense of that many, that it was vast and went higher than the eyes could reach. But the strangest thing was the feeling that I had been there before and somehow knew it well, even when it came alive somehow and it wanted to kill me; I am not aware that one can have a déjà vu experience within a dream without having had that dream before. I'll need to check on that. Mostly we don't remember our dreams and cannot call them back willingly, so I must have dreamed this before or some fragment of it touched a nerve and that fragment—" She shushed my lips and her smile said she understood the shards, and I rolled up into her and held her and we rocked a little to and fro, then rolling into the gasping arrangement of parts. After, the morning got busy with a dozen phone calls and while breakfast simmered, she showered and I listened to voice mail and learned that I was on the front page of the Times, proclaimed a hero.

"Your ship has come in, dear Randal." She wiped an omelet onto my plate and then came back to hold my head in her lovely hands. "Now that you're a hero, we can finally get started," she said. I dismissed her remark as *whatever* because I wasn't sure how I felt about it: someone had snapped a pic, and to become a paladin of the press in this town means the cretins come calling along with those that mean well; I've seen it happen before, and the best laid plans of mice and…well, I've spent years building the credibility of my practice, a statement all phomorphs can lay claim to, and I hoped to ignore the best of this and just shine it on down the road. Before I kissed Claudia farewell at her stop, we had picked up the paper and sure enough, there I was with the recumbent jogger whose grey sweats so blended with the sidewalk it seemed his head and limbs emerged from the cement like a hatchling.

Most of that morning I fielded phone calls full in the knowledge that if I didn't there would be no peace at all but rather a seemingly endless lineup of malarkey, media, and morons.

"Poe, I been trying all morning, this is your friendly neighborhood precinct calling."

"Good morning, Detective Kearns, keeping your powder dry?"

"Well, I wanted to say congratulations but also warn you."

"How is that?"

"This could get ugly; people will think all they have to do is say the word *vowels* like it's some kind of magic mantra where instead they'd need the Heimlich maneuver, and pronto!"

"Well, then I believe it will be in the best interest of all the friendly neighborhood precincts to put the word out," I said.

"One other thing, do you know the meaning of the term *photobomb*?"

"That's a new one on me."

"It's a creative way of spoiling a photo-op at the last second, either by leaping into the frame just before the shutter snaps or by posing in such a way that the person taking the shot is unaware of your presence."

"Okay, but I am not at all behind the eight ball here, so if you wouldn't mind—"

"Well, you've seen the Times, they're all running it, the photo, and here's the funny thing, when children grow into adults, they don't look the same, do they Poe"

"Well, I am not detecting whatever it is you are, detective."

"Don't get snappy. Look again at your now famous picture, the crook of your elbow. That Ms. Roget got in there isn't the question, it's how the two of you did it that wrinkles my brow. Call me when your conscience is ready." Then the phone got busy again, but I let it go on ringing as I retrieved the paper and took it with me to the kitchen to get a cup of coffee. And there it was, or she was, and my mouth dropped far enough to have admitted a plastic bag. As I knelt on the sidewalk with my hand on my thigh, in the ell of that arm held akimbo appeared a tiny face, unmistakably that of a girl, yet her features were mature and her eyes were looking not at me or the jogger but directly at the camera that had caught the unforgettable likeness of Claudia Roget. I called him back.

"It sure looks like her, doesn't it? But there was a crowd gathered, some kids too, apparently. Listen, the reason I called is, it had slipped my mind earlier, this man has been following her around and when we tried to confront him, he took off, and we followed him." I gave him the address.

"What is it you want, Poe?"

"Well, for starters, find out who lives there." He snorted.

"Don't pull my chain. People that live in the Theatre District don't do B & E in their spare time, anything else, like what you and Roget are mixed up in?"

Book Two

The Legend of Hyperbole

Chamois wasn't in when I arrived but his door was ajar (on the first day he'd issued keys to this ground floor den and study) where we could await him, so I edged it open and peered inside the realm of the great one, almost hoping I'd catch one of the tubs rifling drawers so I could use the conflict or the guilt to build a story. In an alcove off the main room, three walls were tiered with framed photos of what looked like art deco and others with a few celebrities sprinkled among them revealing our host at gala events. These I gave the once over as I examined the others more closely. The artwork wasn't thematic and yet each was emblazoned with a message with juxtaposed graphics and it took me a few moments to realize they were ads, pictures of ads for a wide range of products from ketchup to luggage to tractors. The other wall held books, many by the man himself, some with cracked leather spines and once gilt intaglio covers and musty, crumbling frontispiece. Among knickknacks along the top shelf, a green glass marble the size of a tennis ball that held within it, a smaller blue one like a miniature planet Earth. Twirling it gave me an odd sense of elliptical slippage in a flash that was gone as soon as it came. Between the shelves and a desk stood a hat rack on which draped a cloak, a cape, and a long sequined evening gown, the baubles winking as I ran my hands over the fabric. Well, his walk alone gave him away, not that it mattered to me; more power to ya, pal. The main room that he used for lecture had presumably once been a living room or a den for the bay windows gave onto a small garden to the side and partly the street in front and admitted quiet light. I stretched out on one of the couches to await the arrival of the others, and soon

discovered the room had been lit with candles and sloped gently toward a distant speaker, robed in ruby velvet and who stood behind an intaglio lectern heaped with scrolls...But these things, as I said, don't at all concern me, who indeed am not prescribing how one should write and speak, but am pointing out what to do for training, where, as everyone knows, all things ought to be exaggerated. Then I am instructing youth, in whom extravagance of speech does not seem wrong to Quintilian, because with judgment, superfluities are easily restrained, certain of them even, age itself wears away, while on the other hand, you cannot by any method cure meagerness and poverty.

Now if there are any who fully approve the Homeric Menelaus, a man of few words, and who, on the other hand, disapprove of Ulysses, rushing on like a river swollen by the winter snows, that is, those whom laconism and conciseness greatly delight, not even they thought to object to our work, for in fact they themselves would find it not unprofitable, because it seems best to proceed by the same principle either to speak most concisely or most fully. If indeed it is true, as in Plato, Socrates acutely reasons, that the ability to lie and to tell the truth cleverly are talents of the same man, no artist will better compress speech to conciseness than he who has skill to enrich the same with as varied an ornamentation as possible. For as far as conciseness of speech is concerned, who could speak more tersely than he who has ready at hand an extensive array of words and figures from which he can immediately select what is most suitable for conciseness? Or as far as concerns conciseness of thought, who would be more able at expressing any subject in the fewest possible words than one who has learned and studied what the matters of special importance in a case are, the supporting pillars, as it were, which are most closely related, which are appropriate for purposes of ornament. No one certainly will see more quickly and more surely what can be suitably omitted than he who has seen what can be added and in what ways. I felt a squirming at my feet and looked down to see a dwarf Claudia in a tiny monk's cowl staring up at me and I shot up so fast I got a round of applause from the tubs, displaced from their davenport, who hovered bulbous, vulpine over me.

"So, where is she," said one. "We know you saw her."

"You were with her," spoke another.

"We saw you. Then we saw her but for a moment."

As I arose to confront this rudeness, there was a crack like a thunderclap and the tubs vanished, and I was alone in the lecture room but for the setting sun and the vestiges of a dream too vivid to have been one. How long had I slept, and where was Chamois? I had my answer soon enough when my cell phone beeped. The message read: Apologies for the surprise, but I've had to go out of town – back after the weekend, Chamois. I sat and let the dream wash over me. Claudia was so real, even as a dwarf there's something too familiar, far less an auricular whisper than a creased membrane. Was it the photobomb? Kearns' rudeness had surely trumped my heart, and it occurred to me how perhaps I had been chivalrous, laying a cape over the mud of denial like a Raleigh to his Elizabeth. There's the rub, love truly is blind if doubt is a cyclopean third eye, opening like an oriel in dear Love's pate to spy my lackadaisical approach to lasting romance. And I thought then of Button, as wild as her mountain, and then of my first, a truck stop stripper. I stood up and stretched and prepared to go when a bar of sunlight caught my eye in the way it angled into the alcove, and I walked through it and sat in the writer's chair. After reminding myself that ethics is a series of absolutes and that such principles must never be tread upon, I began opening the wooden drawers as others opened and shut in my head: this is wrong; are you crazy; what are you doing; STOP it right now! I listened to the conscience choir and sat back. Would he have willingly provided keys to a group of strangers if he had left anything of real value here, I reasoned, and though it rang hollow its echo stayed with me long enough for it to seem at once a familiar and defensible line of reasoning. In the fading light I opened the large double drawer and the files suspended there held documents of onionskin and handmade papers browned and brittle to the touch. To see them better I was tempted to turn on the light, but then his neighbors might also be aware of his absence, so I demurred. At the back of the drawer was a small rectangular wooden box. I lifted it out and opened the lid, noting it was hinged along the back, and withdrew the folded papers. It was a standard residential lease but it was the address that stopped me short, that is short of yelling Geronimo! I tucked the document into my notebook, put everything back where it had been, and let myself out. As I made my way to the subway in the gathering dusk, I tried to connect the dots. Claudia, that is Roget, (there were now two women with that name) had been followed by a man who we in turn had followed to an address on W. 48th in the theatre district which was leased to a Baroness Mrs. Claudia Von Dusenburg, an unusual name and, could it be, none other than my cross- dressing patient, even in a city this size? The lease to said house was somehow in the possession of my fiction-writing teacher, although the lessor's name was that of a holding company, and I would need greater powers to get any further: Kearns, if I could somehow get him to help. He thinks I'm up to something unsavory, or we, rather, but maybe we can feed him a nibble, something to motivate him, but what?

2

I got home that evening and saw the newspaper lying on the coffee table, notable because neither of us subscribed, and I rarely bought one these days. It was the Times with the front page missing. I found her in the kitchen making a cup of tea. We hugged, and with my arms encircled, I said:

"That picture in the paper, pretty remarkable huh? We should find that kid and adopt her; I mean the likeness is truly incredible."

"That policeman was here, wanted to know what was going on; he's rather persistent, you know." She broke my grasp and took her tea to the table.

His presence explained the newspaper.

"You spoke to him. I want to thank you for standing up to him."

"He called from here?!"

"You must know that I tried to show him, but his second sight is sealed," she said.

"Show him what?"

"He is a sleeper."

"He sees too much if you ask me, reads augury between the lines" I noticed a corner of folded newsprint sticking out of her blouse and plucked it out and spread it on the table. A crease ran through her face marring it some, but she covered it with a hand and said:

"He must have been following you."

"He can follow me all he wants, it's what flat foots do, and where they got the name, I imagine." But I remembered that I needed his help and that to get it would require some bending of the truth; I would need the pretense of a caper yet feed him something viable.

"No, I mean him," and she pointed to a bystander, just another face in the crowd. "He's grown a mustache again; it always makes him more visible, I thought Dughall had better sense, but I think he's lost that element as well." I grabbed the sheet and peered at the face and thought that I recognized him, or rather, that it was a face I had seen, that it was somehow familiar, a composite of several faces with familiar features. Had I seen it before? I closed my eyes but nothing came. I then knew that if I continued to look at the news photo that the face would become too accommodating and before long, I would swear it was my brother. We began preparing our dinner and not saying much, but as she set the salad bowl on the table she said:

"The detective won't be bothering us anymore; I sent him away."

"You sent him away."

"Yes, and with a twinkle in his eye." I didn't know what she meant, or did I?

"You didn't, how can I say this… no that's just, no, you didn't, did you?"

"Randal, do I detect a hint of jealousy, American style?"

"That's not going to make him stay away, *au contraire*, he'll soon be back panting and sniffing for the barbeque!" We sat down to eat.

"I haven't the slightest notion what you mean, and I didn't do anything you wouldn't do if you were able. I just sent him on his way and that's that. Please pass the lemon and vinegar."

I decided not to pursue the matter of cracking the code, an ageless chore of dubious achievement given the shifting sands of the feminine psyche in the winds of Time, the winds that also spin Fortunes wheel and propel us all to our destiny, for better or worse. Instead, while I ate, I pondered how I might entice the detective to help solve the mystery that had wrapped itself around me like a vine. If only I knew more, then it seemed I could maybe say that what Dughall was after was instead a rare diamond or some such and maybe suggest that the break-in was directly related to the theatre district house and that perhaps there's an international diamond-theft ring operating from there and that the writer's group was a front for fencing the stolen goods. It seemed a logical enough thread until I edited out *if*, *maybe* and *perhaps,* for Kearns had already shown he was adept at ferreting out bunk. After loading the dishwasher and cleaning the counters, I sat beside her in the living room, now restored to its previous state, lamps on tables instead of the other way around.

"Claudia darling, I feel conflicted. As you know, I want to help you, help us solve this thing with your uncle, and yet I feel somehow a vague surety that it has all happened because of me, due my position as a phono-morphologist, a snug tenon into the mortise of your need."

"Good thing Chamois isn't here," she said, and we laughed, but mine was forced.

"I want to know for one thing, how you did that," I said, indicating the Times.

"Randal, it appears a child was there who bears a resemblance."

"Well, no, an exact likeness really, a twin, except that proportionally she'd be what, two feet tall?"

"Posh, now come closer and snuggle in."

"It's just uncanny, I can't shake it. Who is the kid?"

"Go there and knock upon doors if you like."

"Claudia dear, doesn't it strike you as bizarre that you've been followed, house-wrecked, crank-called and then after all that your mysterious uncle turns up in a crowd that includes a miniature of yourself who is looking not at the camera as it first seemed, but rather at Dughall. You—the miniature, the waif, whoever, spotted him, and I think you know where he is. Do you want to let me in on this? I really do want to help, but I'm tied in knots." She frowned and seemed to look through me. I plunged on.

"Let's face it: you looked me up, seduced me thank you very much; it was the sweetest act."

"Not quite, I didn't seduce you. When you fell on me in the museum, I must say, I was charmed, after which we were on a collision course."

"Well, it doesn't matter who lit the match so long as we keep the fire to ourselves, not be led astray."

"Do not males steal that fire to ignite every skirt, rutting along like dogs; it's forever been that, I assure you."

"Well, I'm not a spokesman, some maybe, but women fall prey to mercurial fantasies that suddenly outshine all else when a hunk walks by, like, say, a cop."

"Why is it you males have this predilection for the prurient?"

"Well, when a guy falls in love, he wants it to be safe, but he needs it to be secure and when it isn't, when his love is dancing the dog, when she's riding the bologna pony and under his own roof to boot—well, it all comes down to that, doesn't it?"

"I thought you had better sense," she murmured, rising to look out the window. "You don't believe me."

"It's not that, look, I'm just saying that (what *was* I saying?) – it just seems that I'm not completely in the picture, you know, a mule without portfolio, and while I have assisted when I could, it has been you, really who has orchestrated the search for your Uncle Dughall who has now surfaced but more so because of me, it seems, rather than you, although he surely has known how to find us. He destroyed this place looking for I cannot imagine what." I almost slipped and mentioned what Kearns had told me, that her apartment had been broken into prior to our meeting, and why I didn't I'll never know, but maybe it had something to do with the trust I thought I was conveying, when in fact I was already suggesting a role for her, one that I was loathe to fully clothe and character for what it implied as to my own role, and yet I felt I was drifting ever closer toward that shore. And in all, I was further conflicted in that I sensed she knew this, and how could I even broach that? For all my education and training, I felt like a mumbling sap. She sat down again and drew me to her.

"Close your eyes and I'll kiss them," she said, and I leaned back against the throw pillows and felt her lips caress my eyelids and then the *wind blew harder still and I saw through the crenellated wall a great maelstrom of blowing sand, a cloud of swirling burnt sienna like a vast swarm of bees as it passed over and so uncovered entablature and slowly then pillars came into view as though rising from the sand and so exposed a temple quartered by marble arteries lined with statuary and as the sky cleared and light returned grasses grew and flowers bloomed and trees shot up like geysers and riding on air he saw it now from above for there were people moving below, unfurling their robes as the sand fury had gone and so utterly exposed an Eden, busy about its business. Caravan debouched at the foot of the temple steps and the goods were carried within; stacked batches of flowers tied with reeds, richly embroidered silk carpet; ranks of swaying amphora strung on poles were hefted up the grand stair as a raft of geese winged in and as they fluttered closer were not fowl but a squadron of avian women and they escorted us, I couldn't see her but I knew she was there and below us now a great pool ringed in columns, a pool within the temple, escorted to behold a dais and a couple standing upon it and I sensed I knew them and I wanted to reach out and hold them but then I saw them as from below. Kairos arose from the depths of the sacred well to surface within the ring where sat her Lord Titania and upon her left hand the king. On the vitreous surface of the pool played the histrionic ventures of the messengers: in glory as guides of the pens of the bards and as muse in slumber they sang and to the morn washed the color of the dawn only poets see and a renaissance of language winged new horizons of the faery Seership from sea to shining minstrelsy—but even then the Elders noted the flight dynamic of Hyperbole was errant, the wing work flawed, something was awry, and down the ages they witnessed the firmament unravel: in folly as she flitted in Hyperbole's wake returning every pinch and pilferage until the day she lost him in martial human cast—those undulant furrows that rocked across the whorl became the Napoleonic Wars—until she caught him, but he adept now at cunning and deceit birthed of himself a contiguous sprite, an embryonic cousin no less dastardly so that each new forfeit and theft brought conflagration, terra horrific, as grew his, now their lusts for the argot of battle, but of consequential chaos they cared not. Kairos at last able to turn his flank for weak was he from birthing and the half fey spawn no match for her prowess, and fled did he from the drums of a new republic divided toward peace and the resumption of a role since outdated, outdistanced, and ever lost. Titania was speechless but not her mate who thundered: I will have the ne'er-do-well gaoled in the Cyclic. She let him spume until spent and counseled: Better for all the Mirlin, and transported thus to distant realms; let the Brownies have him. Kairos will return for Hyperbole but as for his egglette the Cyclic will do and thus brought hence to me, to us. Her wisdom settled him and they bid their messenger fair flight.*

I came to in one of those wide-awake sit-ups as though shoveled out of sleep, but Claudia was already up. Later I remembered that morning's ablutions in precise detail, then repeatedly combing every filament to find the missing part, the wrinkle in the face cream, the cause for Claudia missing and gone away; the note was of little help and remained a signal source of woe; I would read it again and again not thinking there was something missed, not thinking of her not here, not thinking eventualities and absolutes, mired in diction and transfixed in prose. I was at an utter loss why she'd written: 'Randal, I need to sort some things out and if later, I will see you, perhaps, but will know you and be with you,' but it wasn't her handwriting. I called Melody and said I had the flu, and then I ran to see Kearns.

"Do I know you?" he said.

"She's missing!"

"Sure, see the desk sergeant."

"This has gone too far, it's serious now!" and I grabbed the chair back and swiveled him around to face me, my hand in his face, and in an instant, I was hurried to a holding cell where I sat for three hours before I was escorted out of the precinct building convinced that Kearns hadn't been bluffing; he hadn't recognized me. I had no idea where to look for Dughall and my thoughts then of wandering the streets in search of her were honed more sharply when they carried me into the alleys we frequented between the flower stands and the coffee shops, grottoes on the southern edge of Central Park where the Essex looms like an index finger over west side pages, and where one day, how many days later, I stood in clothing I'd worn for a week, and I was thrown back to when my main squeeze in grad school had, on a whim, taken an overnight invite Tar River party-boat to Beaufort and was gone four days before she came back drunk as a simile.

3

I stood all that night again beneath the awning of our building unwilling to yield to a moment without her, but just as unwilling to be alone in the empty apartment. Then, with the dawn, I creaked off the doorstep and headed for the Cumberland, a boutique hotel down on its luck, where I would shower now and then but mostly lie in the dark and stew about failed love; was this love or just misery come to visit: it's been a while, thought I'd stop in and help you review all of your dead-end affairs of the last twenty years, a welcome sop, and Button Springfield particularly, although the sound of her voice was long gone and for a while the pantomime played, reel upon reel, until she morphed with the sense of Claudia, or transmogrified as Claudia's voice coming through Button's gestures, and so I hit the streets again, returning every other night until I lost track, but the apartment windows were ever dark, and it was roughly then I went howling her name through the tunnels and the open streets where I'd already been over the ground; as you walk one way a shadow may pass behind and your turning toward it is a miss by a mile, and so I tracked and re-tracked our neighborhood and then enlarged the search by area, block by block, stopping in familiar cafes and bars for refreshment before doubling back, not ever going too far before returning to peek in again, but lively conversation withered at my disheveled intrusions and often I was refused service: you here again, get a bath you bum. There had to have been something she said, a turn of phrase, a colloquial Briticism of great import, an impacted statement that went over my head, caught off the qui vive, or was just lost in a shuffled decoding of the feminine lexicon; I knew I would find it, and too find Claudia there if only I kept on and stayed true and believed and continued to believe, even as I wandered into well-known watering holes, sat crunched at the end of the bar, convinced that my stink was remorse against an otherwise overwhelming evidence of homelessness, knew that her presence was near and that I would meet with her. Instead, one fair night I ran into Melody and her beau and learned that I'd not been gone for the five weeks I had marked, prowling the haunted avenues, worried and vexed, dirty, unshaved, sleeping in flea bag hotels—none of that?

"Randal! You look worn out, but you have only been gone two days. We, listen when we—"

"Two days! That's crazy! No, it's been—Look, she ran off; left a cryptic note; no farewell, my love, nothing, nothing but her scent and then that gone too, just as completely gone as yesterday. So, I'm looking, searching everywhere and—"

"You come with us, Randal," and as I babbled on I let them lead me away, in utter disregard and only listening in part, but at least what I *did* hear drew me, one filament at a time, a little further out and away from that wallow within, that glue pit of sorrow, and I began to sense the shadow of the desperate two-faced caring nature of obsession, that what drove it like a piston was instead but a scrim, an ethereal façade that fell away to expose its pretense, that faux aegis that sputtered without its props of pity and remorse and so became not ghostly but actual, human, real; the obsession real, oh yes, but little else.

In all, it took about a week before I was back and picking up particles of my livelihood, but even so, I still couldn't get it through my skull that my life on the streets, my dredge of sorrow and lovesick misery, my slide down vagrancy lane, had all been a movie in my own cinema. Claudia was gone all right, no doubt about that, vanished! But the rest of it hadn't happened, none of it! I worked at working to keep alert and stave off what I sensed as a blue funk lapping at the edges, a lurking something dark and dreary that went by a name I didn't wish to acknowledge that I knew, something more ominous than that of love deserted; a dream creature that manifested as *the show* and allowed its eidolon a serial reality all its own, a succubus of sanity, oh man! I left the office twice that first day in order to run down the ten flights of stairs to the street and back again as fast as I could do it. But when I couldn't stop the thing creeping closer, I went in without knocking and flopped in the easy chair in Melody's office.

"You're looking better champ, I gotta say."

"You're the one here that looks like you belong, like you fit. Me, I don't know," I said.

"We can talk all you want," she said.

"It was just—I don't want to dwell... so vivid! You ever awakened from a dream that was so real—no, that's not it—so actual and emotionally true for its context that you went around for days thereafter stunned by it all, even as it gradually faded?"

"And not wanting it to fade, trying hard to hold it dear, right up front," she said.

"Yes! Yes, that's it."

"And with every chunk of it melted, you feel a personal loss, well, I don't want to diminish it for you, Randal, but such sequences are fairly common, are they not?"

"It's not just me, or you and me? No, no of course not... I can see that, this happens to everyone, for dreams *are* magical aren't they, so much so they consume us, or we're consumed by them."

"And usually, we wake up and can't remember a thing, right, not so much as a whisker of the giant cat we rode to Amsterdam; the kiss of the peach; the aroma of grandma's dumplings."

"Mel, you're great, you know that?" I laughed then, more of a squawk really, but the first humor I'd felt in days and not only that, but I felt or rather sensed those edges receding.

She came around the desk and sat on the arm of the chair, took my hands in hers. "You can't always walk away clean Randal, but you walk nonetheless, right, and you keep going because you must. Love is the biggest, baddest beast out there when it turns on you, instead of turning you on, which is the way we think it is supposed to be, and it takes real strength to go on, and you've got that kind of strength, those qualities come through in you every day I have known you."

"You know, it's odd, but I don't blame her. I don't even feel badly about her, or even too bad at all, anymore," I said.

"What a relief, I was going to have to call Dr. Lyfe." That earned a true laugh, one that burst out like a shot.

"He'd put me in a can too, wouldn't he, right along with the vowels."

"Randal's Vowel Soup, the newest in Campbell's line."

"Speaking of tureens," I said, "how about lunch?" With that we headed for the street, and I think I left behind the shade of the man that had entered that morning. She wouldn't let me pay the tab and we bickered or dickered until enough was enough. Then wending my way to the subway, I stopped twice, jolted by an immediacy of memory, too distinct and aromatic to have been else, and I named each place like an owner and then grieved for its loss in a flash, a morsel of grace that surged and fizzled. When the train reached my stop, I knew I needed help with this; counselor, heal thyself. At the corner, if I took a half step left, I could see our windows, where I had stood for—well, it was too much to bear again, and turning away from my block I headed across town but then stopped, turned back and went on home. It was going to be a long weekend, but apparently, I needed the rest.

4

The following morning while I chopped veggies and cracked eggs, I reflected on the oddity of all that had happened lately, going over the parts and pieces and trying to see how they might fit. It was obvious that my writing teacher was connected to or with the West 48th Street address and that someone there was connected with Claudia, and then were the cops, of course. After washing the dishes, I stuffed my pockets with pen, notebook (the purloined lease within), phone, money, shades, and an apple and headed out. It was a nice day, so I walked most of the way. I've always enjoyed walking in this city when I have the time and the weather is fine. I stopped at a book stall and gathered a used paperback. At the corner of West 48th a figure was standing about where I'd thought I would, lingering by a tree where I wanted to linger, but when closer, I sidled up to him.

"Well, I'm happy to see I finally aroused your interest," I said.

"I know you?" He turned to look at me and his wedge-shaped inquisitive face was scruffier, his gray eyes troubled. He hadn't known me at the precinct house which still seemed so long ago.

"Ah, Detective Kearns, always a pleasure talking to you." He stood closer.

"You *do* know me, then. Good, you've helped me out. So, I *am* a cop. The badge in my wallet, I guess it's mine, but it doesn't connect. Driver's license, other cards, I don't know this guy. My face there, sure, but it's like I don't remember anything I'm supposed to know, and that's an assumption."

"Okay, so you hit your head or something. Have you seen a doctor?" Claudia's remark about him no longer being a nuisance surfaced.

"Tell me who you are."

"Poe, Randal Poe. You interviewed me and my—Claudia Roget, ring any bells?"

"Claudia, Claudia, yeah… I think I know that name… say it again."

"Claudia Roget, witty, leggy brunette, British." He grabbed the lapels of my coat.

"Poe and Roget… yeah - I think - I… man this is weird, yeah, okay, you, you were burgled?"

"Now you're getting it, and both of our burgled and trashed apartments are in some way connected to that house over there, and why we're both here, wouldn't you say?"

"I just got back from Florida; went to an address I found in my wallet—my parents; really odd being there, house I grew up in and not recognize a thing, or some things seemed familiar but not connected, down there a whole month."

"Look," I said, "I'm not blowing smoke up your hole, but I spoke to you in person about a week ago." While he let that sink in, I thought it sure was bizarre how time had looped the both of us, extended our lives in a dream state so real that it was cinematic, like striving to reach for the clouds but then upon waking, you find you are taller than before, but then only to discover at some time later that you've been walking around on your toes; or like that old joke you dreamed you were eating a giant marshmallow and in the morning your pillow was gone—but it's on the floor.

"Oh man, four weeks condensed into one? It's just not—what about this tan?"

"You were brown as peanut butter the day I met you." I told him where he worked and his partner's name and every other thing I could to bring him around in hopes of generating a link to his presence there, and lastly, I told him the case he'd been working on, our dual burglary, and while doing so the door opened across the street, and I almost leaped when Mrs. Dusenburg stepped out and descended the stairs to the street. I dragged Kearns behind the tree and she swept by, regally I might add.

"You see that woman, she's connected to all this, to your memory loss or whatever it is, and we need to see where she's going," I said.

He looked doubtful but stumbled after me. We reached the corner and saw her get into a cab and then we tried to hail one but got no response. Her cab was at a light one block up, so I turned and ran, and he ran after me. The light changed and they moved off, but then a taxi came out of a side street and whether or not he had regained his sentient self he flashed his badge and we jumped in and away we flew. Mrs. Dusenburg took us across town to a brownstone building that resembled a Masonic Lodge with its crenelated roof and parapets. The marquee announced a lecture that I'd been invited to, so in we went.

The program told me where Norse Charlton had earned his doctorate and that his scholarly interests prior to the publication that led to his recent career change had been Medieval and Renaissance England and, oddly, the American Civil War. But with a Ph.D. of my own, I knew all too well how odd it really wasn't to have a wide-ranging set of fingers arrayed in a host of inconsonant pies. And another seemingly odd duck was the cross-dressing Mrs. Dusenburg, but a scan of the audience failed to place his or her whereabouts before the lights blinked and began to dim.

Charlton took the podium and thanked the emcee and the funding organization and then went through what we already had in the program, perhaps to ensure his audience that he was well credentialed to speak on the topic at hand. I had my notebook out and ears attuned for bilabial glides.

"Good evening, ladies and gents, it is nice to look out here and see a full house, for my lecture series has been drawing, shall we say, a breath of its own. If tonight be like many others so far, in attendance may be legions that have risen on both sides of the divisive fence that borders my theoretical base which, it seems, has ignited a firestorm and emptied many a chair, including mine, where now another holds the department reins and thusly reigns supreme. So, let us enter the realm. As noted in your program the title of this lecture is, *The Great Vowel Shift and Modern Myth*, so let me just jump right in, as it were. I won't belabor you with the historical facts as we think we know them, as those may be obtained by that opiate of the masses, Wikipedia, the scholar's scourge, or some other contemporary callow catchall, but rather state that this phonemic phenomenon continued well into the 18th century and was carried forward not by a shift in pronunciation but by a shape shift in the position of the faerie kingdom in relation to this one. Scholars have persisted in the belief that pronunciation changed without there being any impetus for it to have done so, and will argue until they are blue in the face, but I stand firmly to deliver us from this disambiguation. You see, the impetus was that Faerie messengers, although not messengers in the purest sense, sallied forth from the Egerian Forest—and let me state here and now that my critics have decried the location of this wonderland as loudly as I have cried for its preservation; they have soiled me with soil samples, tested my patience with test-less denials, bested me with best left unsaid expletives, or so they think, but these lands are diffused, dispersed, and distributed, vasty beneath their ability to perceive them, for on a single clover or a leaf of grass there lies a kingdom greatly diminished for it has always been so and it shall always be, a diminishment of grandeur, the paltry sublime, sublime refined in runnels above the tunnels of love an ant would squint to behold; beholden to you I submit that these gardens spread o'er all of merry Anglo land

and for soever have—and from them our little envoys, if you will, have, as I said, sallied forth into our world to enliven the arts across the vast and discursive landscape, not so much as to improve the often sketchy discourse between the two kingdoms, but rather to shape it, for its former ameliorative inter-relational nature had rusted, as it were, and its consanguineous history was at stake." Kearns' dumbstruck visage earned him my Blackberry. At our next session, I'd remind Charlton that presenting a paper to room full of academics is one thing, but something like this needed diglossia: a lingua franca, the language of the laity. The speaker must have been reading my mind.

"...and as such the morphological relationship had altered as it was meant to and so in writing. For one, we left behind the language of Chaucer on the road to Canterbury and hooked a left turn into Shakespeare Lane. Our little messengers were indeed quite busier than bees, and it is remarkable to note how much was accomplished by so few for so many and in so little time; but that phonemic shift became for one of them a playground of mischief; how it all began I have yet to establish but suffice to say that dipthongs were no longer the oeuvre of one of the sprites. Now, to digress a bit I will attest to those new here tonight, the king and queen of the fae folk had sent forth these two sprites to aid and abet mankind's somewhat withered appreciation of the worlds betwixt and between, for their common tongue had become quite abominable, and which you will find the subject of chapter three in my book, available in the lobby at a very fair price.

"At any rate, no longer satisfied with drawing vowels and so forth, one of these two sprightly sprites began plucking morphemes, and it is conjecture that this purloinment was indeed yet another diagram of the broader plan, shuttling suffixes from the Cave of Voices, shall we say a verb, the third person singular *telleth* had its *–eth* removed; this was also a period that noted the introduction of *–ings*, the continuous ending already a staple in the Underworld. All this was good and well, but then, somewhere along in what we understand as the Augustan Age, humans undertook to improve the language. Perhaps you are familiar with Jonathan Swift? It was he who condemned the use of monosyllabic words. I believe this and other initial movements toward a codification was inspired by the one sprite, who having had fun for centuries flitting among the phonemes and carting vowels hither and yon, took it upon himself or herself, for sprites are not bound by gender but rather can be hermaphroditic, one or the other or both, to collect, for lack of a better term, morphemes and to horde them for reasons which I am on the verge of discovering, but all the while, the other sprite, sent along as chronicler and sidekick, replaced each one of them behind his back, if you will, but so trusted one the other, that throughout time was this chicanery trailed across the centuries and paeans were sung to them, honorarium decreed and coins minted with their likeness. This little larcenist, as it were, never suspected a thing, or did he? By the time of the subsequent series of lectures that begin in November, I submit that I will have solved the mystery. Now, just let me say that these thefts continue to this day as does their rescue and return, and there is a very good reason for the latter: each word that exists in time is itself a piece of Time, a particle. As you would remove a single shard from an archeological site, the amphora from which it came will never be whole, and so is the wholeness of Time disrupted, and I might add, it is a dangerous game for our children and for the children of generations to come; the removal of any particle in the whole of Time will engender wrinkles or waves that propel onward to a pejorative payoff; take away but one of them and centuries onward that wrinkle denudes a sea or imbues a hominoid species with telescoping tripodal appendages, or a sloth in his pulpit preaches St. John of the cross; it couldn't be any other way. This, my friends, is what the sprite has in store if he or she gets away with it even once, though little aware of it she be. This, your wonderful world, will wax and wane and wolves will walk where wise men won't." Wow! I scribbled like mad for his voice had begun to rise and its emotive pitch altered the tone of his bilabial addictive splurge. I would have been recording him but for Kearns scrolling the OED on my Blackberry.

Charlton went on for some time painting a canvas of horrors, a verbal Hieronymous Bosch, of a future denuded by morpheme theft.

"As some of you here tonight are aware, I am in contact with one of the sprites, which one remains a mystery, although I have my suspicions. As far as I am concerned, my somewhat former academic reputation notwithstanding, and one which I intend to revive, the sprite is a primary and valid source, one who has, to quote the bard, 'a mint of phrases in his brain,' and one who has permitted me the opportunity to see down the ages as no mortal otherwise has. To that end, I remain the foremost authority on the so-called *late* Great Vowel Shift and its implications for all of English-speaking mankind. Belittle not its littleness for it is bigger than your ability to perceive it, and bigot not my study for it as well is grand. Now, behind the curtains here you will find sofas and chairs, coffee, tea and light fare, if you wish to participate in the informal Q and A, for it is a hallmark of this lecture series. Thank you, and good night."

As the lights came up and the audience rose, I saw Mrs. Dusenburg making a beeline for the stage as others also headed for the stairs and moving into the aisle to allow for passage in that throng, I thought I saw Claudia but then was fighting the tide in the aisle and back pedaling to the exits and after a dozen thrusts got me nowhere, I found egress by stepping from one emptied seat to another, leapfrogging the rows, and soon Kearns was doing the same.

Behind the proscenium hung with its heavy velvet house curtain, a traveler by the looks of it, I encountered a melee in tweed and chenille, and I caught another glimpse, Claudia that is, those prominent cheekbones, that nose, and leaving Kearns at the refreshments, I headed further upstage and into the left wing while also catching glimpses of a past not plumbed in many a year; the theater I had been impelled to as a kid by my playwright father but which I later fell in love with, for certain a better home. Well, that got shot down when I failed to gain entrance to college, got kicked out of the house (theater of the absurd) and had had to make it on my own.

I stood on the stairway leading down to the dressing rooms and listened: whispers emanated from elsewhere, and creeping about I discovered a janitorial conference in the Green Room. I retraced my steps and returning to the stage, a crepitating clatter drew my eyes upward and from somewhere on the bridge, up there in the flies, she said *hello lover*, and I raced for the ladder, but once I'd gained the walkway, all was still. I thundered the length of its galvanized steel gratings and found nothing and then went back again, puzzled and haunted by what, another mirage, an auditory hallucination? Then the strangest thing: a thrumming near like a hummingbird so close it seemed to snag my ear and flitting past I turned to follow and made for the ladder and shimmied down.

The stage was deserted but for Kearns chatting with caterers and then I glimpsed Mrs. Dusenburg heading to the back stairs, and I followed her and came to a doorway leading onto an empty hallway lined with storage and dressing rooms, voices coming from one halfway down. It would be crass to say I tiptoed, but soon after I stood just behind the half-opened door in the tenebrous glow of sconce and listened to the voice I'd heard in my office and earlier on stage, and another I knew even better.

"You went well beyond what we had agreed upon, my friend."

"My dear, he simply needs to get it doesn't he?" Charlton's voice cracked and he sounded less certain than during his lecture.

"You got carried away, again aloft with your fine ideas," hissed Chamois, or was it Dusenburg, their voices aligned in that similarly inflected British English, register approximate.

"But you forgo the *ownership* of those ideas at your peril, at ours together, or do you forget?"

"I was doing that for *him*; your job, you promised to do that."

"I have been quite busy, you should know."

"You break all your promises!" They'd moved closer together and I strained to hear.

"Now Norse my love—"

"You swore me Egerian Idylls, but since then I've seen only the ruin of my academic career, reduced now to lecturing to –"

"You must be patient; she must be stopped for the agendum to be drawn."

"I found her for you, a mere mortal, and you, you…."

"You don't listen, I told you—lost the ability, not as do *you* but an ocular sense of her shade's aroma, for eons had I this, but no more."

I don't know if it was fresh paint or the dust-down on the floor, but I sneezed before I had a chance to catch it and then got smacked by the swinging door.

"Who's there, come out!" Chamois loomed.

"Well, well, if it isn't the struggling novelist."

"So, where have you been" was all that I managed to produce from a multitude of questions swirling like a menagerie. His weekend out of town was how long ago?

"You are as cheek and fresh as ever; I know what you're going to say; but listen to me, never abandon your characters. The very suggestion of legging it, of vacating their tale is too fine a shave beyond preposterous, a haircut beyond fiasco." This didn't sound the Chamois of old.

"Have you an ague?"

"I'll pass on sass," he said, unscrewing the fettered cap of a pocket flask and swilling likely half.

"You know I can't always—"

"Follow?" His eyes drilled mine and I had trouble getting my breath.

"Live two lives or three even, though I need to –"

"Ah, that's not it you see; we are all many parts of one entire, why, emotive streams—"

"But wait, you see, there's so much going on."

"Yes, Randal, and you grasp it and run or wait for it to come around again."

"Okay but it's not writing I'm—"

"Once you *have* good characters, or halve them, to make a pun, you must deliver them, as it were, but if you let them go, they will step right out!"

"Well, there's just too many things going on, too many hats in the ring!"

"You have got to hang in and hang on or you may get hung! I can assure you, Randal, there have been numerous cases of writers abandoning their characters, leaving them to their fate, although *their* as a pronoun is as indeterminate as it is user specific, you can see problems surmounting."

"What are you saying, really?"

"Can't you read between the lines, morpho-boy? Why it is unspeakable: shadows created in one genre appear as manikin wearing toilets in another, doused in curry and cornflakes, quoting Robespierre…" and he removed the familiar box of Gauloises, withdrew a cigarette and lit it.

"Well, I need to see Charlton." He smiled.

"Gone, I'm afraid."

"But I just heard the two of you."

"Eavesdropping, are we? Well! Snooping into private affairs, for dialog is it—yet another no-no, my boy. I can see that in my absence you have become ever more the amateur; without my lantern upon the path, you are stumbling on roots: how do you expect your narrative to follow if you cannot?" A door closed somewhere to the left—Charlton? I sprinted to the end of the hallway and up the steps, but whoever it had been was gone, and when I returned to the dressing room, so was Chamois.

I don't know why I went around switching off the lights but at the next room marked Wardrobe my heart shot into my mouth and wedged: Claudia stood there leaning against a walk-in closet, smiling. How long I stood there gaping like a geek I'll let the reader ponder, but soon enough we were hugging and twirling like Velcro dervishes; it was all the language needed in those speechless moments when time itself was at a loss for words and the scripted silent suffering of my five-week hallucination evaporated. I stepped back and looked over her floor length frock and bonnet and tried to gauge the century.

"Looks like you've been to Mayfair."

"Well indeed good sir, and a luscious muffin have I for thee."

"Strike that tent, and I'll butter it up!" Scurrying beneath the hem I headed north as the frock twirled about me, and tantalized by the gyre of heaven's own puff pastry, I arose beneath the whirring hoop of the skirt like a hovering bird as we strode arm in arm through a summer wood beside a gurgling stream that I sensed I knew; was it familiar or was it love that cast an ambrosia of the spirit. I drew her to me and the dress came off; she giggled bird song, drawing me down, stripping my clothes and taking me then, and the sun behind my eyelids and the breezes on my skin were as nothing of compare. We lay together nuzzling and then slept, and then dreamily I came awake to note we were in a honeysuckle copse. Claudia awoke, kissed me, and said, come along, there is something I wish you to see. I looked once at our clothing on the ground and then followed her into the woods. Soon again, I heard the gurgling and we came upon the stream and followed its bank beneath the weeping fronds of willows where it curved around a fallen tree, then opening on a broad pool that I knew without the how of it. On the bank we hugged, and then holding hands vaulted into the pool where we danced and flopped like children, yet also like those grown enough to couple on shoal. In the woods again, the sun dried our bodies as we approached a tawny brick wall, and seeing it, touching its surface I knew it, knew that down it several paces was a rusted gate, and it was there alright, although this day its wrought iron folium glistened as new and sure enough on the other side stretched a broad shaded lawn which led to the secluded side of a grand old manse.

5

We stood together and watched gardeners work among islands of azalea before we strolled unseen across the lawn and up the back steps and into the kitchen. Ah, but it wasn't a kitchen, and yet I knew that this room would become one, and Claudia smiled and squeezed my hand and we went through swinging doors and into the dining room and my gaze traveled up to see the whole chandelier there, generations before a kid with a bb rifle would pluck its cut-glass orbs. On through the library we swept, and I sensed the need to stop and soak it in but was propelled forward and up the grand staircase, down which a butler descended without so much as a by your leave to our endishabille presence. She had my elbow when we reached the top landing and steered me right when she knew I would instinctively go left toward the sanctuary of my old room. We stopped in the hall and she measured my confusion with kisses on lips and eyelids and put her tongue in both my ears and then holding hands again we went through a door, and I didn't blink that it was a closed door; but it didn't matter, because he lay before us fully dressed on the four-poster atop the counterpane with his arms folded across his chest and a smile on his face, a withered version of my own and of one who now came into the room with a woman dressed like Claudia had been. We followed them into a blue anteroom streaked with sunlight. The man laid a leather-bound tome on a long table and took the woman's hand.

"Thus, we have each and every piece specified in the testament," he said.

"Of these I am familiar, but not so the book."

"Darling, it is not so much a book as it is a collection of orders."

"Orders? You said a book."

"Military directives given by officers; I don't doubt that Old Man Lee's are in here somewhere along with a host of lower ratings." As they spoke I moved or was drawn to the table, then hefting the calfskin folio and turning to Claudia, but my mother stood in her place and the room was now my attic cove and distantly I heard my father's vocalic bellowing rolling barrage of vitriol, such a constant in the life I'd lived long ago, so ancient standing here, so dusty and mildewed that I began to mist and mom held me then and when I cleared my eyes Claudia removed the book from my grasp and returned it to the table and again took my hand and led me back, but not as we had come; we lurched into frames of location without traversing their distance, suddenly the yard, the gate, and then the woods and anon we came clothed through a wisteria grove that framed a corridor at the end of which stood the open closet door in the Wardrobe room of The Larkspur Theater.

Without a word Claudia changed into jeans and a T-shirt while I stood by like a rank actor who'd gotten his cues mixed up, scenes jumbled in him. She held a finger to her lips, turned off the light and stood by the door. There was no sound to be heard other than the low hum of the building and the city outside it and she took my hand and led me up the stairs and sat us down near the top. I felt giddy.

"Randal, do you understand what we have witnessed?"

"No, I mean, well, how did we, no, not completely but I..." I was so whelmed I couldn't—words swarmed but failed to slot into place; my larynx felt packed with honeycomb, my trachea raw with unshed tears.

"You must resolve to stand firm; do not permit encroachment; you must dissuade all notions of trade or transmission; nothing can be given you that will equal what you abandon if you allow it." She held my hands and looked into my eyes and I heard her voice say to stand with her and stand fast and our love will be eternal, and the measure of it went so deep that I plumbed it that instant without a plan, just straight down into the heart of the heart of it but was annoyed when, cut that out, someone was already there to interfere, shaking me, and I sadly broke away and sat up and looked into the face of Detective Kearns.

"Ready to go, sport?"

"Go?" I looked past him and saw people chatting in small knots as the caterers boxed their wares.

"You look like you need a drink," he said. I gave him my hand and he hauled me up and we left the stage and went up the aisle, and I didn't turn to look back, fearful that the whole of it would shimmer like a summer horizon. Had I seen Claudia?

A block away we stepped into a bar and I sagged into a booth and ordered beer and it went down so fast I ordered two more.

"What happened? I'm beginning to unthaw, it seems. What happened to me?" said Kearns.

"Well, I cannot even begin to explain because, oddly enough, there are no words in the lexicon for doing so. But it seems that similar or coeval elements are at work in me as well or at least smoldering therein."

"You're the word man, Randal. As more of it comes back, I make the connections between things, simple things I would never have thought twice about before; I don't know whether to be pissed off or thankful," he said, and slugged his beer.

"Anger would have no focal point, nothing to zero in on, be thankful your dose or whatever, you see what I mean, is not what I'm dealing with."

"Yeah? Well unload on me and let me decide." I didn't know where to begin.

"It's like this woman I'm in love with—"

"That'd be Roget, right, you see, clearer every minute." I guess the combination of the edge in his voice and his flippancy at tossing off a name that was dear to me rubbed wrong, but there was something else nagging at me, and I saw what it was, or heard it rather in the palatal medial consonant of her lovely surname as my tongue lightly caressed the roof of my mouth: Roget… Roget… Roget.

"You there Poe?"

"Just drifting."

"You were telling me about her."

"Oh man, well… I really don't know how to phrase it. Unlike any other woman I have ever known in any capacity, she—Claudia has the ability to send me into these, call 'em what you will, hallucinatory dream states—"

"She dealing drugs Poe, that's what you're telling me, like Ecstasy?" That did it.

"No, but you are, I believe. Another strung-out cop, except your narcotic is stupidity, and I can't think of a worse addiction."

"Hey fuck you, huh? I get back into shape, twenty-four hours maybe a little more, I'm gonna arrest your ass. I told you before whatever the two of you are mixed up with is quits, but you don't listen." With that he got up and walked out, and I sat there and calmed down and then got dreamy again and after a while and another couple of beers, I asked the bartender to call me a taxi and he did, and then asked if I needed one sent.

6

At home I hauled a wooden stool into the shower, too tired to stand. The spray fell in a cascade of crystal droplets smiling and winking as they plopped and pattered and sang their rinsing ditty while effluent whorls of ardency also swabbed and at last, I emerged pink and sparkling to the core and saw us crossing the lawn in Umstead Mills and wondered if I couldn't just go out and order a steak and champagne, wander across town in the buff. I was now drip dry and put on a robe and made a sandwich and a mug of tea and was partway through them before I became self-aware. What time is it I asked, and knew before the thought passed that it didn't matter, that I had to go to sleep, that I had to get up and go to work in the morning, that I would need to be coherent, and at this last wisp of consciousness, I began to weep.

It had been a long time, and at first, I had to let buried thoughts and emotive shards work their way to the surface like soil erosion. Had those flings in grad school been anything greater than stress relief; those of us unmarried may well have been studying the field in our *spare time*, a phrase I'd picked from the first doctoral student I'd swooned over and bothered to no end, a gorgeous articulate. But I had remained mostly single throughout it all, then a sole doctor with no one to applaud his elevation. Further back then, skipping over random dates and hasty mates and the course went straight into the Appalachians where a commune still lay in its emerald nest; where a feisty and independent-as-all-get-out girl, woman I should say, young then, probably still young, tied herself around my heart in a bondage of adoration. Love, that hardest of words to define, the easier it gets bandied about the harder to sense its core; in the end its truest expression is limited to a woefully inadequate store of morphemes, and why centuries of endeavor have yet to hit the nail on the head. Was I in love then? Absolutely lost and confounded within it, and where later I emerged lost and confounded without it, and while love arranged time to suit its variegated nature, in hindsight it's all over and done with in a flash, visionary one moment and sightless the next, in thrall in a prison of joy and devotion but suddenly pardoned to a desolate freedom. Okay enough of that, get me away, fly further back, but there was little, I knew, of true love, if ever I'd had an inkling of its nascency, it was short-lived in my life so far; my parents had seemed devoid of it as though two comets had collided and produced a haphazard rendition pretty much left to arc its own tail through the sky. What to do? I had drawn myself far enough back from the loss of candor that is also love to know I was afflicted and in a dire way, but where was the object of my ardor, was *where* a place or another figment that could only be reached while holding on to her, touch making the physical real? I sensed the worry this could bring because it had the same flavor as my faux five-week nightmare of desperation, but it flitted away, shoved aside and run to ground by a stronger sense of purpose toward a fidelity of trust. And with that I turned off the lights and made my way to bed.

At the office the following morning, I whistled my way through piled up correspondence which included another offer from the persistent Dr. Lyfe, but on this day, I found not a whisper of a problem with his proposal and smiled through the reply. Why not? Melody strolled in.

"What's with the flowers?"

"Huh?"

"What's the occasion?" I'd forgotten about my call to FTD.

"'The rose looks fair, but fairer we it deem / For that sweet odour which doth in it live.'"

"Well now, and you do look rosy yourself today. Was that Marlowe?"

"Right country, right century, wrong poet," I said, again whistling. She planted a hip on my desk.

"Randal, males don't just quote poetry."

"Well, you know, the sensitive ones do: Mermen; brawny meadowlarks."

"Phillip Sidney, I'll bet."

"Put your money up, for 'when daisies pied and violets blue / And lady smocks all silver-white / And cuckoo-buds of yellow hue / Do paint the meadows with delight.' I'll bet lunch that you'll miss your guess."

"You are in love! Tell me, when did you meet?"

"C'mon, play your part."

"Who is she—it couldn't have happened at a better time; you've been so down."

"Well, I've known her for months, actually."

"What! No way, Randal, you *wear* your heart—I'd have known. So, the two of you have just met; tell me where?"

I couldn't remember… was it a face in a window, a shopping cart encounter, an errant Frisbee? What I was certain of was that I'd known her intimately for a long, long time. But then I remembered when Melody and her guy had rescued me that I'd been unable to coherently frame a synopsis of my loss; I was so stuffed up I couldn't see straight. And now, how to own up that I'd bought flowers for a figment?

"Guess."

She took my hand in hers and kissed the knuckles.

"I am so happy for you!

"You won't be happy buying lunch; I'll eat a horse with spite and horseradish."

"You will tell me when you're ready, I know. And by the way, if you're going to gamble, you need to be crafty."

"What's that mean?"

"The first one had me and you might have stopped there, but I sense Olde Billy in the scansion of the second, and hah! by the look on your face, I know I'm right. We'll dine at, let me see, Brother Jimmy's."

"Yeah, right, not on our combined salaries, we won't. Besides I have a two o'clock."

"Males do, however, renege on their promises, quoting or not."

"You're serious!" She headed for the door, and I threw up my arms but followed.

"Come along, Casanova."

7

That afternoon I met with not only a new client but an addiction not on the books as far as I knew, and although homophony (their, there) is familiar territory to many, I would submit that its pop-culture vernacular misrepresentation known as *mondegreens* is not. Simply put, a single morpheme may have two distinct meanings such as *club* as truncheon or *club* as social guild. In English there are countless examples of the homophonic but few of them really noteworthy except to those involved in second language acquisition. I would submit that its cousin, the vernacular misrepresentation known as *mondegreens*, are far less common because they're a feature not of the oral but rather the aural. The term originated in a memoir that had appeared in Harper's Magazine in the mid-1950s. As a child listening to old ballads read by her mother, the author wrote that she built a world of unrequited chivalric love based on the phrasing: They have slain the Earl of Murray and Lady Mondegreen. In the ballad, *The Bonny Earl of Murray*, however, the speaker despairs of the Earl's murder after which they laid him on the green. But a more contemporary variety has become quite popular: song lyrics. The example with the widest familiarity is from a Jimi Hendrix number in which the phrase, *kiss the sky*, is often heard with the final three free morphemes merged as *kiss this guy*. The two-o'clock had asked me if I was familiar with it, and before I could frame a response, he played us a tinny version from his I-pod, although I heard sky not guy.

"But that's not the, not mine, not why I'm here, you see."

"Some are catchy enough to snag the unaware," I said.

"I mean that one; I think they're all from 20th century music. But I'll tell you, my father and me we were always at loggerheads, never saw eye to eye, well, I guess that's too far back, but anyway it was left up to me to go through his stuff after he died and I'm sailing his LPs across the room like it's Ultimate, you know, Beatles, Stones and all this ancient stuff, tossing it out there at the dumpster we rented to clean the place out. Then I get to some discs I'd never seen before and start playing them you know, this old turntable thing, just one song each and then wheee, across the room, with it. I slide out this record, guy named Sam Cooke and then I heard this thing and ever since I… I can't get it out of my head—no wait let me finish. It's more than that you know, it's like I'm even writing it, I can't write anything else, just this thing over and over and over and when I run out of juice and wind down, I play that song again," he said.

"Well Damien, let's start from the induction point, the lyric itself." He keyed the I-pod and we listened to another hit sound of the sixties. My familiarity with the singer was thin, but this was all about listening to the lyrics, and then I heard it: the singer or the song's protagonist finds himself in a nightclub or like venue and he's dancing a very 1960s dance, the twist, with a woman who's wearing pants, then called slacks. He switched it off and sat pop-eyed, and then burst apoplectic: "It's the chicken slacks! The chicken slacks! Dancin' with the chicken slacks, the chicken slacks, the chicken slacks, dancin' with the chicken slacks!"

"Okay now—"

"Look!" He pulled a daypack from the floor and extracted a sheaf of notebook paper on which he'd penned line upon line of *dancing with the chicken slacks* in a cursive that began neatly but style-wise deteriorated to a scrawl near the bottom. Beneath those papers were other documents, such as an auto-insurance application form for policy holder Chicken Slacks. But I didn't let that distract me, for I had noticed several things. My own -ing predilection had zeroed in on the missing final 'g' in the verb, dancing, and though it took some doing to get him to acknowledge it, let alone begin using it - he'd been writing it but then dropping it verbally, and the change was dramatic for its pronunciation lengthened the verb's medial syllable within its constriction of air flow and seemingly made it a new word - but at the same time, I knew that alone wouldn't shake him completely loose. Another thing, and perhaps the most important, was the utter lack of context, for the addictive phrase had been sheared from the lyric whole. Lastly, the sexism of *chick* was so outmoded as to be almost lethally ridiculous.

"Damien, have you put this into practice?"

"I don't get your point."

"The dance itself is what, fifty or more years out of date."

"You don't… like… no way."

"You have nothing to lose and much to gain," I said, and got up and went through the connecting door and into Melody's office. Soon, the two of us returned with her music rig and while she set it up, I opened the cornucopia of You Tube, and the three of us watched twisting on the desktop.

He blanched, but Melody coaxed him to his feet, hit the play button, and we were twisting the day away! It took less than three minutes before he reached out and hit the stop button.

"Excuse me, but this is like the stupidest thing I've ever done."

"Not a dancer."

"Dance!" he snorted, "that isn't dancing, it's like slicing a loaf standing up."

"You are free to disagree with it on any level, but you and Dr. Ungwen here, this woman in pants - you were *dancing with a woman in pants* (if she'd been wearing a dress, the analogy would have had the day off), you got that? Let me hear you say it."

"The woman in pants?"

"That's it, again."

"The woman in pants."

"Okay, now give me the whole phrase and with danc*ing*."

"Okay, dancing with the woman—there's no ring, it doesn't..."

"Say it!"

"Dancing with the woman in pants."

"Are you? Tell me."

"Dancing with the woman in pants."

"And Damien, tell me, who wears slacks anymore, slackers?"

"Remember the people in the video, those were slacks," said Melody. "They had a comeback in the post-punk era, as I recall."

"Yeah, wow, and *those* guys are circling the drain," said the client as he crammed the satchel's contents into the office round file. When at last he swiped his card, it was nice to see him sign his true name before thanking us for making something dire seem so lame, as he put it. We sat around talking after he'd gone, not likely to return, and so garner a nickname, but one never knew.

"You know, he reminded me of the Daffy Dame," said Melody.

"God, how long has that been?"

"We had just opened, I believe, like that week?"

"I mean the lyrics, you know."

"What was it she brought us… Marvell, right?"

"Randal, your memory is top notch. Go ahead now and show off."

"It wasn't even the poem's final verse but rather a poignant one:

"'But at my back I always hear/
Time's winged chariot hurrying near;/
And yonder all before us lie/
Deserts of vast eternity.'"

"And, let me sort it, she had been fired from what, three prestigious colleges for insisting on the legitimacy of changing the scansion to fit her—what did she call it?"

"Rhong Rhyme: in that verse, *lie* and *eternity* are not phonetically rhythmical, so she—"

"Yeah, hah, she was a hoot!" And we would have gone on in that vein if Wallis Fordham hadn't knocked on the door jamb and crossed to the desk. In the back of the flat the elevator wasn't audible.

"Dr. Poe, I, ah, I have had a relapse," she nearly whispered. "I think I will give Dr. Ungwen here a try if it's all the same to you."

"Please, just see me before you leave." I busied myself with tedium by going through the mail, and was writing a proposal ostensibly addressed to Dr. Lyfe when Wallis returned.

"She's good."

"Yes, she is, and also good to have as a business partner."

"She won't..."

"Not unless you request it."

"That's okay then, the dual approach. So, what did you want to see me about?"

"Well, I wanted to ask, given your field, if you're familiar with the work of one Norse Charlton."

"Oh my, what a surprise, by which I mean, I was expecting, oh, articulation, not the least a shot off the wall in left field."

"Mind you, mixed metaphors should be avoided, not counseling Wallis, just advice."

"There is no better way to say it. He is called *Charlatan.* Here is a gentleman that turned scholarship into buffoonery in a fortnight. His primary sources are whispers, glyphs in séance wax, and runes only he can find with a dowsing rod, in a word: malarkey."

"But once a popular academic, it seems."

"Oh sure, yes, solid background, respected; we go back, he and I, same area you know, always knocking into one another at conferences, and we once presented together at Oxford; of course, I was instrumental in helping him gain his late position. It is said fortune often smiles broadest before a backlash; time has eroded the connection. How did you come across him, I'd like to know?"

When I didn't respond a little chuckle warbled out and she scooted forward.

"Randal, just once, once only, break the oath; I *have* to know."

"So, it's fair to say you're skeptical about his current output."

"Tell me; it will never leave this room."

"Yes, but you see neither would I, Dr. Fordham; my reputation would be toast."

She mulled it.

"Well, from what I gather, his printed book sales are destroying rainforest. I won't criticize that, after all few can make a living at writing, much less buy a house in the theatre district and surround—"

"Excuse me, but would you know the house?"

"What? Oh sure, I still get the odd invite, palm readings and so forth, but… association with his ilk these days, word could get around."

"Not scholars I take it." She chuckled again.

"Moondog duplicates, most of them."

"Moondog?"

"An area jazz musician way back in the forties and fifties, I think. He went around Greenwich Village in a wizard's cloak with moons and stars on it, wore Viking headgear, antlers, but unlike these clowns he was an artist who produced real music, if a bit odd. No, the Charlatan's cronies are self-styled seers and mystics that wouldn't know a Gurdjieff from a handkerchief."

"And where did you say this place was again?"

"Well, I didn't, really."

"I thought you had."

"Hmm, I think how odd it is that two Medieval/ Renaissance scholars, once colleagues, would find their way here independently… is it subtle or pronounced?"

I considered her then, even beginning to think like a female, the wily coot, and should have known she wouldn't let it go.

"Look Randal, just between us, we both hold doctorates, a tiny percentage of the population, and as members of the club, as it were, there are things that can pass between us not privy to others, a *gentleman's* agreement." It made sense only after I covered my ass with ethical scree. I told her.

"Indeed, not at all what I expected, not at all."

She arose and gathered her things.

"Now, Randal, if you are in the market for a crystal ball, go online, but otherwise you might try 109 West Forty-eighth Street but here, take this card; it's like an ID bracelet with them, and also take an umbrella lest the gargoyles spit on you from the eaves."

We shook hands and parted on far better terms perhaps than any of our previous sessions; for I think we had reached an understanding that transcended our complement: Ratatat Haha was dead; long live Wallis Fordham.

And that address was the same as on the lease I'd taken from my writing teacher's desk.

8

The email announced the resumption of the writing class that evening, and before leaving the office, I replied that I would be in attendance. I hardly remember it. Tired from a busy day, I thought a hike home instead of the train would starch my shirt, but I was worn even more by the time I arrived with takeout in hand. The door wasn't shut all the way, and I heard a chair or something scrape. Not again! I knew the rule in these things, you retreated and called the cops, but I'd had enough of them lately, so I kicked open the door and attacked with pizza.

"Is that you sweet?" Claudia!? I raced into the living room and stopped dead.

"Who the hell are you—Where's Claudia?" I shot putted the pizza at the man on the couch and ran for the kitchen to grab a knife.

"Randal, it's me! It's me, it's okay, love." Her voice had come out of the guy, out of his mouth. I came back into the room. "I missed you so much," she said, and the guy took the pizza and set it on the coffee table and then came and took the knife out of my hand and led my bewilderment to the sofa, I guess. That part I've blanked on, an apoplectic moment, instant aphasia that occluded also pepperoni and black olive and mushroom. My first words stumbled.

"So… you're really what, a guy, or, no, it's not possible! You're a woman! What's happened?"

"Randal! Well of course you would be surprised, but really! What does Willie tell you, he's arising to speak, is he not?"

"He says that I am in over my head… but in love with Claudia."

"Hold me Randal, here, that's it, the way we have," her tongue swirling in my ear, then my stilled mouth silent as I struggled out of pants and she of hers revealed all woman beneath and we seated the bulb just so and squirmed in that mash that gets it done when probably it shouldn't quite so fast, so sudden, too many other things going on, things that are somehow not what they seem and that no remedy unmasks for rapidly they change again and the upkeep is far too dramatic for your average pedestrian lusts, and there the desperation in lovemaking that contrasts it so with love. We squirmed about on the floor, I with my eyes shut tight imagining Claudia as I knew her, and this was she, no male had that silken skin—my eyes flew open.

"How do you do that?"

"Hmm, it is ever so nice to be with you again, my dear Randal."

"Claudia… oh Claudia, how do you *change* that way, how can you be both sexes, back and forth?" Her eyes closed above a beatific smile as she rolled about, but I had slipped out soft as a gherkin. She was female everywhere but the face, not hermaphrodite… but what? I was in love with a freak of nature.

"Claudia, here," and I held her in my arms and we lolled back against the couch. When I asked again, she stilled my lips with her fingers.

"If I tell you Randal, you must never repeat it, not ever, not to anyone. Promise to me Randal and solemnly so."

"Claudia, I love you very much and anything you tell me, anything at all, I will hold as dear to me as you are; what passes between us is our business and no one else's."

"I will diminish a little even by telling you. It is why I cannot find Dughall; he has bandied too often and become as thin as the air or taken another form perhaps; I have been near him, sensed his presence."

"You disappeared once already, and it broke my heart. Then when I saw you at the theater, I forgot all that anguish—but it was a dream I think, we made love in the woods where I grew up?"

"Dream is a vehicle, a transit between realms."

"It was so vivid, so real, and my grandfather, the same house I grew up in, only—."

She again pressed her fingers to still speech, and said, "didn't that explain it? You all have a pixie form but have long forgotten its embrace."

I looked at her then like I never had, really, not even seeing the guy, just onward into her eyes. "We were *there* weren't we, and for a reason, too. He was dying, or had just died, and all his things from the war were laid out… the cutlass and that folio, is that what I was taken there to see?"

Her voice dropped to a whisper: "Darling, how Dughall got from Julius Caesar to James I to Napoleon – detours to Columbus, Erasmus, Shakespeare, irrelevant to his purposes, for he remains entranced with martial arts on a grand scale, the order that had set in motion corps on a checkerboard, the power in such usage rings still. Does it matter that he was ever lowering his sights, and so following all the way to General Shives Poe?"

"What?"

"Randal, within that book is a threat to all of mankind. You must protect the book lest it fall into his hands… for centuries he has been stealing words only to have his shadow put them back, for unreturned to Time their absence ripples across its whorl, upsetting the course; the more taken and not replaced, the greater the tides' destructive power… dear boy, the tiniest particle removed from the grand continuum ripples forward upsetting not merely the pace of life, but far less subtle are birth defects, abnormal disorders and behavioral proclivities that extend even to your area."

Can one be crazy but cognizant? I was about to find out.

"Too often the swirl of the hermaphrodite cape between acts, and bear in mind this play has been staged since before antiquity aged, hath worn his form to be more akin to yours; a human must arrest him finally: so to your ancestor, so to you."

"Are you saying that Uncle Dughall's morpheme addiction has throughout time, or because of it, actually created and then spread his peculiar affliction within a multiple personality?"

"It is precisely so, pullulatus ultimatus."

I filed the Latin for later and thought of Charlton and his book and heard his voice from the lectern tell of long ago and far away but really very near claimed he, and only yesterday, and it seemed that both his and Claudia's referent was the wily Dughall who must be what, four thousand years old? But that would mean… a sense of righteous denial was barely keeping the lid on a question that I staved off asking by reminding her that whatever was up to me was equally up to her. It didn't engage.

"Claudia, who… who puts them back? Who puts the words back?"

"Kairos," she whispered, her mouth on my ear, "Kairos puts them back, many of them but not all, sadly, and chides him for the deed, for he believes the words he takes have occult power when removed from their beds; and that his collection will grant him ascendancy." Relief ebbed denial downstream, but it was flowing back.

"Do you know this Kairos?"

"Oh indeed, for Kairos is"— a pounding on the door interrupted us and whoever it was kept up its unrelenting boom, boom, boom! While dressing I looked through the peephole to see Kearns pacing in the hall. When was this prick going to leave me alone? I stood still enough to hear the clock in the kitchen tick away its moments and after about two hundred, I eyed the peephole and the testy bastard was gone. And then I had a déjà vu; Claudia would also be gone when I reentered the living room; only the Latin she had spoken lingered in the air along with a distant glimmer on how five weeks had since transmogrified into forty-eight hours and how Kearns had also lost a sense of time and place if what he had told me was accurate. I stood in the hallway, again listening to the clock and arranged as best I could what had been happening, from the dreams, if that they were, to the odd disappearances of my love, to the latest client connection, and then came to and realized that like a mortal I was heading out the door, the apartment's lone entrance and exit.

Book Three

The Ancient Evergreen Maroon

The door to the anteroom was closed and the tubs were already arranged in their tubbiness when I arrived. They glared, diffident or pouty I couldn't tell, and then our host emerged and greeted us.

"Randal, I see that you are without the barest tools of our trade. Where, may I ask, is your notebook? No, no, don't tell me dear boy, respect the dignity of the rhetorical question. Did you expect one of us to supply you with pen and paper, and perchance ideas too?"

The tubs sniggered like beefy chipmunks.

"A necessary element for any writer is the ability to listen; I doubt this bunch behind me has much I can use, but within your speech, sir, may be the wisdom of a river. In point of fact, it's already helped jump start a few stories."

Placated, Chamois placed a writing tablet on my lap and said: "Alright, everyone will write a scenario in which flattery attempts yet fails to win its target. Set it up and then expose it in dialog. While you're doing that, I will make us all a nice cup of tea." He tittuped into the anteroom, and I thought of the box with the musty papers, but then got busy with my sketch.

When time was up, pens down and teacups empty, Chamois went about his business.

"Janet, I said flattery not flummery. Go home and rewrite. Hmmm, Vera wouldn't you say we know all too much about Hercules and the Cyclops to suspend belief that flattery may have given that ogre pause—rewrite." And one by one they tubbed out and it was obvious he was making me wait.

"Alright Poe, let's have it." I let him have it, alright:

"It was in the Hedge Wood of the Egerian Forest that the king and queen of all faerie, Oberon and Titania, argue, and its degree has tilted all of nature and the world slides toward a precipice of discord and turmoil unless one of them be appeased."

"Well, I think you've listened a little too closely to our lecturer friend and purloined his ideas."

"Not at all; why, his own scholarship is flawed. Any Elizabethan scholar would see through the veil the mark of the Bard."

"He would roundly disagree with you."

"Let him. I was going to bring it up at his last appointment, but he failed to show or even give notice."

"Hmm, you will simply need to clarify, talk to him; we cannot have this sort of thing, pilfering of a *chanson de geste*. Now, your dialogue is testy, quite good these salvos, although I'd change the names Hyperbole and Kairos to something modern say, Ed and Thelma." He handed the paper back and straddled a chair facing me.

"This Friday we're having a bit of a fete, and I would like for you to come."

I pulled out my phone and pretended to study it. "Well, nothing's on it seems; tell me how to get there."

"Oh, but you already know, do you not?" and the snippiest nip of the inflected verb said he knew I knew.

Well, I told him that I'd been out walking one day and happened to see him emerge from a house in the theater district, and he let me carry on, smiling all the while, the show bird. Give a peacock a beret and a packet of French cigarettes and what do you get? A peacock.

Once again, I thought of that hanging file of brittle onionskin as he showed me the door and halfway down the steps the thought of another such paper arose, a fragment torn from an ancient document by a gender-switching client who called herself Claudia! No, it *couldn't* be, no… no. I didn't want to believe it, even remotely, a hell of a coincidence yes, but in Dusenburg affectation, body language, and mien rang resemblant in both genders; when you really thought about it, they might have been aphetic twins, brother and sister, siblings taken to wearing each other's costume, acting… but Claudia? I didn't sense her in the guy until I held his naked form, but the vocals, well the feminine register would be pretty hard to guise, and telling me things only she could know, and then of course my ache for her; I saw myself willing to accept her in any form and be proud of that as an accomplishment; if she'd told me she was Hippolyta the Amazon Queen, my love would not waver from the measured, steady beat of an embowered heart, except that it might ratchet up in a Herculean effort to snag that girdle, but that's an altogether different story. But how different really with her as an ancient, an immortal being able to switch genders across the streams of Time yet unable to recognize others like herself in mortal form if what she had whispered was indeed what I had heard. As I headed home, I fought a carping sense that she was using me to find her uncle or whoever he was, and each time the suspicious little hook reemerged, I clung to her, to us, our cuddling forms on the carpet; use me, abuse me, love me; I'm yours! What if she was using me, did it really matter, I questioned, but from that sanctified inner core of conscience came trundling the soft parade of the forms and flavors of trust, each a value greater than the next, but I determined not to listen, smothered it and tamped it all down like a shovel on a campfire and focused instead on two more days, two more days and then I'd get inside that house, invited in, no less.

The following day, due to a cancelation, I was determined to fill the hour with as much nothing as I could fit edgewise into sixty minutes and might well have but for the telephone.

"Good afternoon doctor Poe, this is doctor Lyfe."

"And good day to you too, sir, now as to your business proposal—"

"Not why I called at all, this is a professional concern."

"I'm all ears, how may I help?"

"Well, we have a patient who is exhibiting a form of adult babbling and I wondered what you could tell me about that because there is no evidence of head trauma, no autism, no schizophrenia; he is coherent while utterly incoherent."

"Is the patient a Scat singer?"

"Not to my knowledge."

"Religion?"

"Well, ordinarily we wouldn't give that out-let's see… says he's a Methodist, lapsed.

"That probably dismisses glossolalia or speaking in tongues as it's sometimes called."

"The patient spoke clearly when he arrived but since has clammed up save for random bursts."

"Interesting, and this is an adult, well, as any language scientist would tell you, there's no clear demarcation that separates babbling from speech; it is a stage of linguistic development. The patient could be regressing… I would say right off to listen for labials, the lip-labored stops, that is the stopping of air flow, as these are quite common in infant babbling but have shown a remarkable rebirth in the adult phono-sphere. Is he by any chance a bird watcher?"

"There's nothing in the file to that effect, why?"

"Well, it's a wild shot, but the nonhuman animal model for babbling has long been the song bird and there was a case of a German shade tree ornithologist who took to a form of syllabic mimicry of birdsong and warbled his way into the books."

"Now we're on to something, he did mention butterfly wounds," said Lyfe.

"Butterfly wounds? Hmm, that has to be a first."

"Yeah, but I feel it has sent us down the wrong track because what we're treating him for is Arbuckle's Effluvium."

"I am not familiar with it, but you mentioned random bursts without elaborating."

"Arbuckle's is, ah, well, for lack of a better term, penis snoring; it's a rare form of erectile insomnia, but the science is thin."

"Well, I'd have to concur; I do not recall an iota from psycholinguistics where odd cases abound."

"Before he went cuckoo on us, he explained that he and his wife were producing and selling, let me get this verbatim: wedding bowers, archways formed of hardware cloth on a lattice frame onto which are stapled plastic butterflies, an origami of taut piano wire. One of them toppled, thus the wounds."

"Okay, there go the real butterflies, but that fails to explain the babbling or the snoring lizard."

"Apparently his wedding anniversary, a distraught spouse, psychological distress, and the combined trauma has brought on Arbuckle's or something perhaps akin to it wherein the sufferer emits peeps like a chickadee from his trouser trumpet; that alone would be enough to unnerve anyone, don't you think?"

"Then it is a psych-related issue, a Freudian oddity that must be approached from that area; you are dealing with a form of traumatic aphasia. I can refer you to a colleague," and I gave him the number. We then spoke about our business arrangement and got the ball rolling.

2

From the closet I took a Navy velvet sports coat, a smoking jacket, thinking that I'd go stylish intellectual or casual snob or something crossing those lines, dark purple shirt and black Armani jeans over Wellingtons and I was ready for any theatre district fop gathering. And as was my want, I just began walking without a thought to distance. I like to walk. I'm a walker, besides, the other choices are so limiting it seems, confining. If you don't dwell on it, you can cover sixteen city blocks in no time at all; awareness of time when hiking makes each step a tick of the clock and that alone will wear you out and you arrive a dishrag. I was bounding along in the fine evening and wondering about the attic in the old homestead in Raleigh and Claudia's plea, and so didn't notice when Kearns fell in behind me and kept pace half a block back, didn't notice him even as the door was opened by a liveried butler until Kearns said, "we're together," and with my elbow in a vice he steered us inside.

We were greeted by a beaming Norse Charlton who broke away from a group of men; it was all men as far as I could tell.

"How nice of you to have come Doctor Poe, who is our charming friend?"

"This," *asshole* I thought, "is my bosom buddy, Phillip."

"How very nice to meet you, Phillip, may I call you Phil, and are you also a patient of our esteemed Phono-morphologist?"

"Actually I'm—"

"He's a deliquescent dipthong dabbler and suffers from oxymoronic mania but his current fixation has been metalepsis," I said. Charlton had steered us into the less crowded dining room where a penguin served us flutes of champagne.

"I am not at all familiar with those, and perhaps we shouldn't—"

"Nonsense, Phillip is very open about his illness, and this one is, as Harold Bloom has it, and I paraphrase: 'a word substituted metonymically for a word in a previous trope so that a metalepsis can be called, maddeningly although accurately, a metonymy of a metonymy.'

Kearns glared. Charlton's fixed smile sagged.

"Well, your own Elizabethan George Puttenham explains it quite well in his *Arte of English Poesie*," I said.

"Ah yes, that I should review, and it rather seems that it would be of interest to our friend Chamois, does it not," said Charlton.

"That's why I brought Phillip along; the two of them have a lot in common."

"If you'll excuse us," said Kearns who then steered me into a corner unoccupied by knots of jabbering gents.

"Alright Poe, we're inside your mythical den of thieves, so I'm going to give you the benefit of a grain of doubt from a distant seed in a barren harvest. You go on and play your word games. I'm going to snoop around, but I want to see you before you split, so don't get lost." I too intended as much but wasn't about to tell him, so I made my way from dining room to living room and group to group, alternately introduced or left to my own, and then passing through a set of swinging doors into a large open kitchen, I found a group of women gathered around a teak island which was overhung with cast iron and stainless-steel pans. I thought it was odd that they were here at all, and all in here, as though sequestered, drinking wine among themselves. Moving closer, I spied around the side of a frying pan the size of a manhole cover, a Tarot deck and on them Claudia's hands as they gathered the cards, passed the deck, and withdrew. Flitting between the pans I chased her profile as she sprinted from the room and out a door, but I caught up in a walk-in pantry where in a tenebrous corner she stood beneath rows of dusky silver cans. I eased the door shut. In the gloom her face seemed to glow.

"Claudia! I'm so-*why* are you here?"

"I followed the man that followed you."

"You can follow me—okay which one is he, Dughall I mean?"

"I have told you! I have made it as plain as a pikestaff; I cannot see him in this form."

"Then tell me something else, why has he been stealing words? Intellectual property rights aside, what is the point of it all?" She held me at arm's length, resisting my urge to hug her.

"Oh Randal, you must know then… all right, Dughall flits from one century to another with little care, stationary in this one, for now, but he is emotionally stuck in Time. He became enchanted with himself during one twelfth night and believes with all his heart that he can—that tropes from that era hold great power, as once they did for describing the fantastic, the horrible, the grotesque; they were necessary to that age and we charged into them the popular command and so they transformed culture; it was a spectacular success, but he became convinced of their occult power and he believes that it is the words themselves without any context whatsoever, without human or faerie hand, without smile or kiss, without moon or sun, will alter our world and yours, will change them to one wherein he exerts control over all domains drawn to a design only he can see."

"In other words, he's crazy."

"Randal, you must protect your ancestor's book. I have already seen what emerges there if he is allowed to remove its contents."

"What connection could there possibly be between Elizabethan or Jacobean figures of speech and American Civil War orders and letters?"

"None, there is none outside of his swirling pate; but the issue is grave, Randal. Each theft of his wrinkled a tiny fissure in the pool of all Time, not that which you know, but would have been far more disruptive had I not replaced each one every instance he turned his back to take another. But over hundreds of years, he has been fixated on the martial and that civil engagement of yours is, well, like a project. There is no rationale to apply to his acts but ever so much to apply to yours. Hear this dear boy: life as you know it will cease to exist; none of this will be here and what replaces it I couldn't begin to describe, nor can I show you; I can take you back with me, briefly, but not forward," and with these words she sagged into me and as I held her to me she seemed to collapse upon herself, to grow smaller until it felt as though I was hugging a child, and in the crepuscular room I remembered the kneeling girl in the photo, just as a light came on overhead with the opening door and Chamois stood there appraising me as my eyes adjusted and there was a popping sound like a whip crack of thunder and a blur shot past and out the door behind me, one that led to a staircase.

I spun around, surprised at the double ended pantry, and took the stairs on the fly. When I reached the landing, I heard her voice in quick and bitter argument with another from somewhere down a hall lined on either side with doors. I called out to her while twisting knobs and at last swung one open and she reached toward me with arms like bands of elastic vapor stretched from across the room with her torso distended beyond an interior door and she shrieked as her twenty-foot body whipsawed and with a snap that popped my eardrums—that image vanished and the room lay quiet and empty but for the thumping of my heart in the echo of a scream. Mine? At last, after a split second of telescoped centuries, I peered around the connecting door and found Charlton sitting on the end of a bed.

"Norse, where is she, the woman who, who—?"

"Everything is just fine now, at long last." He smiled.

"Listen, I need to speak with her, it's urgent!"

"There's nothing you can do; she's gone, or perhaps you are."

There was no use pretending. "We're talking about Claudia Roget, yes? I really need to speak to her."

"She's in the mirlin now," and he chuckled. "I was there once too."

"Tell me more, tell me what that is," I said, and slid up a chair so I sat facing him. He made no response and seemed to be meditating or looking beyond me, but if he saw me at all he offered no recognition, and I think I remembered Lyfe just then for the flash of an unethical synapse a half-step in advance of the thundering thought of what I did next, hypnotizing him with the tonal shifts of the once popular but long discarded embedded-word technique, derisively called the *in-bed* technique for its captious misuse by countless practitioners.

"Norse, this is Randal, do you feel alright today."

"Splendid, if I must say so."

"Good, I want you to be comfortable and relaxed. Tell me about Merlin."

"A world inside a world inside a world, it keeps going if you permit it, but one must disengage."

"So… this is a very large place, this Merlin."

"Oh no, Randal, the mirlin domhanda is very small, a glassy sphere, carry it in your pocket if you dare but the careless will find themselves in a pocket within and carried along eons into the bargain."

I took a leap of faith and described the glass ball I'd seen in Chamois' desk, and he got excited.

"Oh! That may be the grace, but there's another, and I have called on it many names in order to sing its praises."

"If you would tell me what it does, we could praise it together, a team," I said.

"It is the domhanda's utility to transport between realms, to the other worlds that are folded within like the leaves of a tome. I know it, I learned it, I was… inside it, if you will, and then set free upon its pathways, free to roam forever if you but know where to seek."

"You got back alright, so Claudia can ah, find her way out?"

"The one you call Claudia is a villainous little seelie banished now far beyond Elysium, and rightly so… we have been tracking her for some time, but it took a fool to lead her to us."

"Who is we, and who led her to you?"

"Why you did, and it all fits so nicely, Randal my lad. I for one am immensely grateful."

I was no closer to finding out where Claudia was in this maze of riddles other than somehow pitched into a marble the size of a plum, a tale not unlike that of the Arthurian Merlin imprisoned forever in a petrified tree. A shiver ran through me.

"Norse, how old is Dug—"

"What is the meaning of this!" cried Chamois, flinging open the door as though the thought of the uncle had summoned him. He glared at me as he helped his friend to his feet.

"Wait a second. Norse, we are concluded for now, and three, two, one, awake." Caught in the act, it was all I could do to make right. Unfortunately, Charlton didn't see it that way.

"You hypnotized me? I'll have your license for this! And every dollar to your name! How dare you! Now get out of my house, damn you!" Chamois scowled beneath the beret.

The party downstairs seemed unaware of the histrionics above, and I found Kearns chatting to a couple in the dining room. He seemed relieved and we made our way through the crowd to the front door and were ushered out. From across the street, I looked up at the windows. Couldn't it be she had really gotten out, instead of miniaturized to the size of an idea? An enormous sense of loss whelmed me then like those haunting memories from irretrievable childhood when trying to measure the ratio of their emotional placement in the stream of time, and I worried that I had done the right thing.

"Poe, you were on the money all along, even if you did lie, lookee here," and he held up a small hardcover book. "Recognize it?"

"Look Kearns, I think Claudia may be in danger, *serious* danger and I—hey, that's mine, that book was given to me back in high school." I palmed it and inspected it for damage and then fanned the pages of the biography of my ancestor, Civil War General Shives Poe, and out flew a sheet of paper. I bent to pick it up. It was my copy of a partial draft of the Gettysburg Address, one penned by Lincoln as he sat in a Gettysburg field owned by a man whose life my grandfather had saved, or so said the lore.

"You told me nothing was missing," he said.

"Who creased this?!"

"What's your problem, I folded it to get it in the book."

Anger flushed my face, but my concern for Claudia was packed around that anger like barrel staves, and we were wasting time.

"Look man, I've got probably a thousand books, some of them valuable, but none of them were missing. Where was this?"

"Both were in the downstairs den along with some items that may have belonged to Ms. Roget, couldn't be sure. What we do have is enough for a warrant."

"How soon can you get it?"

"Tomorrow Poe, now it's night-night time."

"Wait, I thought justice never slept—look, her life is in danger!"

"Not from any of the clowns I met tonight, Poe. What did it say on the invite, wet noodles RSVP?"

"How early can you get the warrant?"

"Poe, I'm going to be back inside that house by ten, eleven tops."

"I'll need to be with you."

"Not a chance, unless you got another diploma for detective grade; don't worry, I'll call you. Go home and get some sleep."

Sleep? I paced all the night vexed as a hammering toothache too far focused inside to grant an outside and all too self-conscious of the looming veil of yet another love, that great rarity of soul-spelling, heart-rending giving flow gone again and tumbled upon the others; all of each love's endeavor lost in a collective misery revisited in the heartache land I had long stayed away from, too delicate, too unwilling to face what I knew to be true: a familial strain of callousness furrowed through me like a rift, a given trait in the hand-me-down chemistry of a thankless father, but the thought of mother caught me short; she as much a victim as her husband, an unwitting mother who gave up her own life to give to another the pathos of personal redemption for the quandary of being; Matilda had saved me more than once, so what trait then but a need to find and locate fault? Well, it was bullshit for sure, but Claudia was not going to be my soul mate and how clear was that, and I chased again to the rafters the encroaching suspicion that she was nothing but a darling nut threaded onto my bolt without a lock-washer. No, she was a woman, a real woman who knew just as they all seem to a little beyond the pedestrian wallows of our sphere, who knew the moon as her mother and the sun as her shadow and the clouds as particles of an aroma only guessed at by guys; she had that sense about her of the timelessness of her journey into my life, one that passed like a glance from a train at houses and neighborhoods and then stopped at mine, a review of sorts, a step back, because a strip of lawn or a sunshade or a red maple caught the eye; she was like that, and on her way elsewhere she came back for me and took me along, and I wanted us to go and go and go and it just isn't right with whatever happens to be so.

I curled into a ball on the inner swirl of the oval rug and sobbed, a fetal fool.

3

Detective Kearns shrugged again. "Like I said, we didn't get squat; nothing to hang anyone on, except maybe you; they seem irate about your intrusion."

I was all dried out and sober as parchment, too analytical now for engagement on anything but facts.

"Then show me what you took from there."

"Listen Poe, we got some women's clothes, see you can identify 'em, but other than that, no I.D. of any kind, no phone, no handbag, nada. Come with me."

In a wire mesh curtained storage area smelling of moldering paper and sweat, he unpacked a box beneath a dim bulb and I withdrew each piece with reverent care until the box held nothing but its bottom.

"These aren't anything I recognize," I whispered. Kearns drew me away by an elbow and steered me back through the busy hallways to his desk and produced a pen and a document and told me to once again write down everything that had happened since day one. I'll get you a coffee, he said, and walked away. As he did my eye caught an object I had seen before. It looked like the big green marble I'd seen in Chamois' desk and instantly fearful that he knew I'd been inside Chamois' house but too distraught to remember I had a key, I glanced around at the other detectives and then palmed it. I sweated his return and ignored the coffee and wrote like a madman; I wanted out of there.

At the precinct door he said he would stay in touch and not to worry, these missing person cases had a way of sorting themselves out.

I stood there for some time, thinking of myself in the third person, the way we report and read about victims. It's not every day he got to loiter on the steps of a busy New York precinct station like a wooden statue, ruminating, but perhaps it was the atmosphere of making right from wrong that steered him from the all too obvious to a more cogent approach to fate, and he drew from his pockets the marble, notebook, and i-Phone and before the day shift and the night shift changed faces for places, he had a plan, and with that he stepped on down to the street and hailed a cab.

I pushed the buzzer, and counted, do it all night if need be. At last, I heard footsteps and was greeted and after a moment, invited in. Would I take off my shoes? Upstairs, I entered a large coffered room rosy with light and broader than the house appeared from the street, lined with tables down the center while armchair grotto lurked in shadows. At one table Wallis Fordham, bent over a folio manuscript like a stalactite, but not so formed, straightened and stood, and victim no more, Randal shed those duds.

"Dr. Poe, to what do I own this, this most uncommon house call?"

"Please Dr. Fordham, I am in des—I need your help."

"Well, the tables turn, do they not, but we know that. To be fair, my friend was reluctant to admit you—please excuse this mess; I have been perusing John of Salisbury's notion of the world as a stage. Well, please come here and be seated. Can I get you anything?" She was dressed casually in shorts and a T-shirt and I tried to keep from looking too directly at the body of this former man who had since become a woman as she hopped about tidying up. Even seated, my host seemed to be wired and in that soft light her ash blond hair seemed whiter than ever, electric.

"Alright Dr. Poe, you have the floor." I briskly related where I had been, and what I had seen and heard the night before. "What can you tell me about the mirlin domhanda, if I have that right?" Fordham crossed her legs, leaned back and stared past me; drive shifted to neutral, and took on a persona previously un-witnessed by her analyst: a woman in her home, relaxed.

"Well now, you've picked a dandy plum with that one. The Domhanda eh, allow me to extrapolate: Norse Charlton and his, shall we say, rooster you've called Dughall, having ensorcelled you in soiree amid the favored Beau Brummels have likewise led you down flights of fancy with a flair for showmanship unequaled since the likes of Svengali."

"You helped me get inside, remember?"

"Randal, fifty some odd years ago we, and I use the pronoun loosely, pulled the same toy wagon across the heavens with magic mushrooms and the tribal jamboree of eastern mythology and it drew a crowd; yet the attraction to theirs it seems is not new age but rather a dark ages counterpoint, a modus minstrelsy—but never mind. We might speak for hours on that topic and never get anywhere but further in, and as such, I'll not tax your knowledge of the era. There were scholars, philosophers that dabbled in—well, alchemy to make short work of a much broader field, whose devotion to God was devoutly Christian—occultism wasn't yet decried as pagan, and yet there was a juggling of spheres as they sought proofs to ancient riddles they believed would instruct them in the utility of incantations to the spirit realm, and more importantly in the function of objects of the mystic arts handed down from antiquity, one such object the mirlin, the Gaelic word for marble, of which you have spoken."

I flashed on the giant marble in my pocket but left it there.

"It's Celt?"

"What it really is will never be known, but the name ascribed to it is the Mirlin Domhanda. In Gaelic it translates roughly to world sphere, which seems redundant. The earliest known references give it as a ring of spheres, one inside the next and so on; one imagines a sort of telescope. It was once the possession of an Irish scryer or crystal gazer, a companion of John Dee."

"There's a name I know."

"And well you should Randal, we have spoken before of your wide-ranging eclectic interests, and it is why I enjoy your company; that is when I am not, shall we say, *performing*."

"Dee was seeking angels, or their language, a universal tongue."

"Yes, but that's not why you are here. How may I help you?" I was instantly conflicted as to how to say it, aware that it was all so, just so, and I couldn't finish the thought.

"You're a bit misty, Randal. The woman in me sympathizes while the man scoffs. But as you know, I prefer the feminine."

At the end of my cry, she was sitting on the chair arm and massaging the back of my neck. "Now, like you've often instructed, let it all out: don't hold anything back."

I told her, stopping only to honk in tissues.

"Well, that's quite a tale indeed, especially in light of Charlatan's extraordinary leap from lofty academe to what many may have misunderstood to be the deep end, exiguous sources notwithstanding. My best guess is your lady friend is likely being transported somewhere, elsewhere; the domhanda is to my understanding not a portal in itself but rather more a cell within interlocking cells, that they may reach into eternity is anyone's guess but the literature suggests the spheres are static until some alignment is achieved, think of tumblers on a combination lock, but that's about all we can surmise. There are implications as well of a component piece; what it may be is anyone's guess."

"I am unable to help her, I can't—there's nothing I can do, a dead end."

My phone vibrated with a message from Melody, the ninth such message from her in the last ten minutes:

'You've gotten the same email message now about forty times, and you've got The Duck at three today.'

"If you'll excuse me a moment," I said. As Wallis went off to make us a pot of tea, I opened my email and noted the addy was not one I knew and the message was a poem which made no sense at all until I scrolled down to the sender's name: Norse. I handed the phone to Dr. Fordham upon her return bearing a tray, and within a moment she had it uploaded the poem to her Mac:

Dear Lover Boy:
Her new address is doubly named
Emptied yet full but still untamed,
Hairless at home among the reaves,
An evergreen that sheds its leaves
Yet wears a beard not French at all
In jest, say most it's Espagnol;
Is where to find your lovely wight,
But hurry lad for Time's aflight;
From This cupola looking north
A gorgeous land of fecund birth:
Away to that somber place make speed
The path is rugged and sore,
Through tangled juniper, beds of reeds,
Through many a fen where the serpent feeds,
And man never trod before.

Wallis printed it and took it over to the table she'd stood at earlier and motioned me to a chair where I looked over my own copy and sipped the tea.

"He is clearly taunting you."

"It's a riddle," I said, "doubly named, empty but full, a paradox inside a riddle."

"Not merely a riddle but one aimed at a phonomorphologist, a double taunt. And yet, something here is tinkling a distant nerve, a faint tintinnabulation." The woman who'd opened the door to my incessant ringing entered and the two spoke softly before the other left the room, giving me a look that said I wasn't welcome, but Wallis smiled her out of the room, telling her, "I am Doctor Poe's patient, and today he is mine; do not worry."

"My sister, she is wary of strange men. Listen, there's a bowl of chicken salad in the fridge and pita bread on the counter. How about seeing to that while I do a little digging."

I made sandwiches and called Melody who wasn't too happy about taking on The Duck, a patient with a deep-seated form of hermeneia, grandiloquent repetition for the purpose of interpreting what's already been said, as though others were not paying attention, but that wasn't all. He was also driven by the Addictive-adjective Slur Syndrome, a dismissive dialog, that rare affliction in which affect was its cause; once uttered, its perpetual self-serving motion was tough to arrest, and when excited, the Duck would slide into calumniation like a trombone, and had done so from almost our first meeting, when we were both patients. That was fifteen years ago and he claimed at that time to be ABD at Columbia. He still does. Further, not unlike yours truly, he interned as a pho-morph, but then wormed his way up on the promise of doctorate any day now and is, sad to say, a competitor. Training is essential, but without the proper credentials he is a faux-morph as well as not a real doctor: so, you get the moniker. This fustian battologer is one of our testiest patients and a hard nut to crack, if you'd excuse the expression. While we discussed our latest efforts and the notes I had made and how best to play it, Wallis reentered the room and winked. Soon I was off the phone and we sat and ate.

"Randal, the good news is our friend isn't quite as clever as he believes."

"The good news, implying—well, it's all been bad so far, let's hear the good."

"Well, the first thing that caught my eye was the scansion, the metric feet; they're precise until the final five lines which don't seem to fit. And it was those lines that had caught at something, the tiniest shard, but I drew it out. Far back in grad school, the early days of Comparative Lit, I examined poets of different periods, looking for parallels, a treasure hunt as it were, or is yet, I should say. Look here, there are fifteen lines and the antepenultimate ones, thirteen and fourteen at least, are pinched, as the Brits would put it. That he'd stoop to plagiarism isn't a surprise, but it still makes the heat crawl up my neck."

"Great, so from whom did he steal?"

"Ever heard of Sir Thomas Moore?"

"He was a Renaissance writer, a martyr?"

"Good guess," she chuckled, "wrong spelling. It's M-o-o-r-e. He was a nineteenth century Irish wordsmith, the Robert Burns of Ireland. He spent some time in the United States and one of the ballads he penned here contains these lines."

"Interesting. I noted *serpent* right away; it's archaic but European, and that goes for *fen* as well," I said.

"Bravo Randal," she said, smiling as she sat down, "what else?"

"Well, reeds, and a fen is what, like a bog, right?"

"Randal, banish these British terms; what would we call a bog?"

"Well, a swamp of course, but again the paradox: there's a rugged path but no one has ever walked it."

"Not so fast, Moore wasn't writing about just any swamp. The poem or ballad, rather, is about the greatest swamp on the continent, the Great Dismal, ever heard of it?" My surprise must have registered on my face for she nodded even before I spoke.

"Why of course, it straddles the border of Virginia and my home state, North Carolina; a scary trove by what I recall; ghosts; pirates; runaway slaves. The whole of it is rich in lore."

"Good, that's a step on the ladder, now we climb a little more." She swiveled in her chair and woke up the Mac. "He tells us that her new address is doubly named and that cements the location: in the 1600s *dismal* meant *swamp*; it's redundant, really." She Googled the swamp and we sat side by side and read all we could, which was considerable, and learned of eighty-five species of songbirds and vast swaths of cedar and juniper and white cypress trees. We also read that in 1763 George Washington, along with some friends and relatives, had formed the Dismal Swamp Land Company and tried to drain it for pasture land, but failed. Which seemed to satisfy: *emptied but full*, and still wild as ever.

We viewed more related websites, one with Moore's poem in silly gothic font, and scrolled photos and checked various links. Then, while Wallis went back to studying the poem, I read on about the swamp's history, much of it concerning the many attempts to tame and shape it, all of them failures, and through it I barely managed to keep at bay the sense of the dread, utter uselessness of ever finding Claudia in that morass. I looked up then and found Wallis appraising me, studying me rather than the poem, and I said I had better go help my colleague with a difficult client.

"You're welcome to stay longer Randal. Your presence here at first ruffled by its oddity but since has had a calming effect with not a single outburst from yours truly." She smiled.

"Doctor Fordham, I cannot thank you enough. You are quite the sleuth."

"So, what will you do, leave Ms. Ungwen in charge and head south?"

"I haven't thought that far ahead, but I will have to try, somehow."

"Yes, and do call me before you depart; I may have gleaned more from the poem." She hugged me before I could react, and then showed me to the door.

The taxi ride was blur and soon I was at the office and just in time to spar with The Duck on his way out the door.

"What was Ms. Ungwen's harangue about, you ask of me? That thrasonical fabulist had the temerity to impugn that the aural perception of others in our rather esoteric circle is understood, an overt action, Dr. Poe. Do you overtly agree? Are you too an auralist?"

"Ah, the oral-aural aspect of nature-nurture's effect on the affects of answering yourself; tell me, do you have two telephones at home? That's too bad, but you can remedy that easily enough."

"Two telephones? What do you mean? Your colleague is addle-pated, Randal, and balmy too!"

My inner voice chided, don't take the bait, but I didn't listen. "Better addle pated and balmy than chintzy, dense and execrable."

The Duck chivvied: "Fickle and grody is this hurly-burly, inane!"

"Ah, but thou: jejune and knotty, lubricious and murky, not to mention noxious, odious and puerile."

"She's queer!"

I steered him to the elevator door.

"I assure you she is not, you repugnant, skulking, tawdry, ugly, vacuous, wanton, xeric-yolked zygote. Think on it until we meet again," and down he went, shaking a fist.

Melody looked robbed of spirit as we sat down, but she bolted up over my sudden need for time off and reminded me that her own vacation, well-marked and openly discussed, was but two weeks away. We sat around and chewed it and chewed on each other a little too over our petty resentments, but finally, I made some calls and then more calls, as well as a jaunt over to NYU and after four hours had cobbled together a cadre of the like-trained to cover first my absence and then Mel's. But throughout all the backdoor wrangling I was testy, for here I was pounding the streets when I should've already been in that swamp—the Sisyphean absurdity of which would come back to me later when I would fully grasp its enormity of acreage—and because of Claudia's warning to protect the family heirlooms, echoed in déjà-vu snapshots of the dreamlike visit to my grandfather's house, my house, and so I flew around town putting things in order and then made one last call.

"Ah Randal, thank you for the call, I appreciate your taking the time."

"I am on my way to the airport, to Raleigh, this evening and then out to the Dismal tomorrow. Anything else you can tell me?"

"Well, there is nothing else from the poem; I'm still puzzling over its pesky details. There is, however, Native American lore that is quite fascinating: local tribes were members of the Algonquian Nation and more specifically the Powhatan Alliance, and so a wealth of oral histories. Among the southern tribes, namely the Chowan and the Weapemeoc, are tales of a spectral tree, just as in faerie lore there were sacred groves of tree-like beings. What I can conclude from it all is that I am coming with you."

"Ah, no. No, I'm afraid not Dr. Fordham, you see, that would not only eschew the doctor-client relationship but stand ethics on its head, what next?"

"All its pocket change falls out. Listen Randal, I have thought this through. That which you needn't have known previously is now of vital import: I knew Norse when I was a man, I mean wholly so, if you understand me, a detail I wouldn't otherwise share, but exigencies prevail. Further, I know him in the way only a woman can, and not intimately now but perceptively. I believe I am the best suited of anyone to pierce this occultist veil he and others are projecting, this hokey shroud of mysticism. Finally, two heads are better than one if you'll pardon the simple homily. If you'd like, I will resign from treatment; that way we'll just work together as friends."

I didn't fight it, sensing the relief of a shoulder to lean on, after all it was a good, solid argument, and so I had the company of a transgendered morpheme addict and Renaissance scholar, and thereafter I never again thought of Wallis in the guise of my most annoying repeat client. Ratatat Haha was truly dead.

4

The Raleigh area had grown so expansively in my absence that flying in; well, it could have been any urban setting, so different from the sleepy capitol of my youth. But as the taxi drew further in, I began to recognize more of it, more of what hadn't changed because I had, and I wondered if our sense of Time was solipsistic when the taxi let us out in front of the house which had sat unaltered on this ground, save the random coat of paint, since 1840. The National Register of Historic Places describes it as Steamboat Gothic, an oddity in this neighborhood, but Umstead Mills had once been a village in proximity to the capitol and not far from the Neuse River, plied by steamboats.

The taxi dropped us at the flagstone gap in the privet, and we stood looking, though my view was freighted with history, and the place seemed smaller, shabbier, but I knew how traumatic incidents could jaundice memory and trace poisons linger. My companion gave a rambling assessment of the sheer amount of frilly gingerbread trim and dizzying array of lacework on the three-storied monstrosity with its wraparound porches and the widow's walk that collared the top floor, where I maintained an apartment. The current tenant soon arrived and we shook hands and exchanged pleasantries.

"Wallis, how are your knees, you're in for a climb."

"It is remarkable to imagine you growing up here—it has such a fairytale appearance."

"Well, that appearance is but another façade," but I saw that saying more could only lead to an explication of my dysfunctional family, "not unlike this scrollwork here that follows the stairwell all the way up, or down." We reached the landing where an emotive flash came and was gone before I knew it: this had once been the attic and I sensed its refuge, for it was here I often hid from the raging bull of my father, and here where I had forged a plan to screw him so thoroughly that he would ever remember he had a son, yet one that went awry and caused his untimely death. Its sense of safety had led me to convert it into an apartment while the lower floors were rented.

I gave Wallis the brief tour and she decided tea might be had in the micro-kitchenette, and I went into the alcove (an apt word to describe the whole of it) to find the trunk pulled away from the wall and where it looked as though someone had tried to pry loose the hinges, the padlock bent but intact. Soon I had the folio in hand, but upon rising, I noticed one of the leaded panes missing from the oriel window above, and standing on the trunk I found glass on the casing. Perhaps a bird, but someone had been in here. I called downstairs.

"Why yes, Mr. Poe, perhaps it slipped your mind, but we sent an email when it happened."

"What exactly—I don't recall it."

"Well, more than a month ago, I think. We heard what may have been squirrels or something. They do get in under the eaves sometimes. When it didn't let up, we decided to play it safe and called the police. They didn't find anything amiss. Squirrels or pigeons I suppose."

"There's a broken window, a small one up there—if you'd call the maintenance." I sat down with the folio on my lap and thought of Claudia reduced to the size of a gnat—could Dughall exchange his size at will, shape shifting between hominid and honeybee? I eyed the window. Can a honeybee carry a pry bar?

"Cozy is the word for this place. Imagine being young and in love, this is the perfect garret," said Wallis, as she brought in tea and we sat and looked through the scrapbook, a moldering folio filled with all manner of items pertaining to my illustrious ancestor, including a receipt from a well-known national bank for the security of… the Gettysburg Address? Was it an original from which I had a copy? I couldn't recall the details, and so I got out my phone and called my old mentor and friend, Tarleton Ramseur. After pleasantries and our bon mot badinage, I inquired about the document.

"It's funny that my old brain is called upon to remember what your younger one ought."

"Yeah, well, the known copies are in D.C. They have been catalogued to death. How is it that another exists and more so that it belongs to me?"

"To the estate my boy; do you not recall that as your legal guardian I had power of attorney, and in such duty, safeguarded all you had left after the courts made short work of you? Perhaps it is an occluded chapter, but at any rate, along with that seminal document is a prolix longhand account of the means by which your grandfather acquired it from a Gettysburg farmer whose life he had saved in July of 1863." I scanned the page before me and it was not the full statement but between the blotted lines the gist was clear.

"So, what I hold here is a mock-up?"

"You were off in graduate school at the time that we discussed turning the house into a museum; the state had considered the house for the registry of historic sites, the status attained by my former home, as you may recall. So where was I— the contents of that trunk and of a decrepit portmanteau we tossed are copies or facsimiles that would have been displayed; the originals are held in acid-free humidity-controlled polyethylene sleeves in a vault a mile thick." I thanked him, relieved that I didn't have to inquire if the adjective 'all' was missing from the line that ends: 'created equal,' and marveled for a moment that I had been in that farmer's field, if only in a dream, and promised to visit soon. Claudia need not have worried over those papers; a bug-bomb bank job couldn't free them.

Sitting in slatted sunlight beneath the oriel, Wallis appeared oddly insubstantial like an ephemeral membrane outline, but I rubbed my eyes and reflected on my chimerical existence in this garret, how the spirit of all that absence might seek a continued erasure of all who enter here.

With nothing in the cupboards, we ordered pizza, and I scoped out what further info could be found on the swamp and printed it, notating the margins and the maps, while she buried herself in some books she had brought. "Now, that's interesting." I looked over.

"Yeats makes reference to a sacred tree, a grandmother of the sacred groves, a purported gateway of sorts to the faerie realm. I have followed the reference as best I can and get this: it is found in fens and is said to tower over all. It will take further digging to uncover more if more there be."

I returned to the map where the eye of the swamp, Lake Drummond, kept drawing mine away from canals that ran like broken spokes on a wheel. The canals seemed logical because like avenues they gave access to remote areas and I needed logical consequences to follow sequentially from problem A to solution B, but that eye kept drawing me back, that tannic oval, that ring of water.

"Randal, now don't cry, it is going to be alright."

"Ah, I'm not crying, it's these contacts, got built-in washer wipers."

"Come on now, we will find her."

"Oh Wallis," and she squeezed my lips shut and hugged me, turned my head toward her and brushed her lips against mine, tilted my chin and slapped my face!

"Harold Christmas! What the—"

"You stopped crying; it dried right up! No, listen, wait and listen, Randal. You need to be ready for whatever this is—it is big, this swamp alone, this job of ours, this puzzle to solve, it is already a Gargantua and Pantagruel episode, is it not, and yet we are in it, full throttle, or I am anyway."

"What does that mean?"

"Randal, as a male—no, that's— let me start over. Women are just more in tune with life's inner rivers than men could ever hope to be; we know each other kinetically at a depth that allows us to reach across, how can I best say it, realms of beingness."

"Well Melody—Ms. Ungwen can take over; I don't have a problem with that."

"Randal! Heavens, you're both off topic and singing its chorus; should I slap you again? Look: what you need to understand is that women intuit each other and sometimes the flow between two becomes one; it can happen anywhere and at any time, but when one is, say, more receptive to the other, at times when we are open, souls bared—am I getting through?"

"I'm not sure I follow."

"Look, I admire your therapy, your methodology, well mostly anyway, the lines you follow have worked well, but I have to say, Randal, that off task you're a bit of a drudge."

"Hey now, you've been trying to tell me something and that's clear, maybe I suspect what it is, but I'm not wholly prepared for—"

"That is precisely what I am telling you. You must be fully prepared, morally, ethically and spiritually for what*ever*, for the *even*tual, because we are about to enter the un*known*, or some aspect of what we can name as that."

I got up and went into the hall and emptied the closet: daypacks, tent, an old ice chest that smelled like bad bananas, and a pair of boots, and flung it all to the couch.

"I'm ready."

"No, you are not. Sit *down*." She took my hands in hers. I yawned.

"Randal, the reason I changed my sex was because as a man I was far too dense to appreciate the emotions that ran through me like tides; but since the operation I have—well even the personal "I" of identity has melded, perhaps molted is more accurate in the chrysalis of this new being; I can see around corners, hear colors, yes, and as you know, hiccup morphemes, but it seems, at times, that flows more from your office, almost from you."

I yawned again, unable to follow what she was saying.

She stood then and drew my hands to her breast. "Randal, *your* Claudia and the "I" that has become the new me are riding a wave, and we would not have met without your helping hand; you brought us together." I don't know how long I stood there after she said goodnight and closed the bedroom door; I may have slept standing.

The following morning as we loaded the car and again at the Kroger, I felt half of me grab a sack and the other half stow it; my love for and adoration of Claudia had been halved and so, self-consciously and with two minds, one navigating, the other drove down-east heading for the Chowan River crossing outside Edenton where I'd once scrubbed a sloop's keel in the brackish Albemarle Sound as eerie weeds slithered my legs, the duty of a regatta rail rat. Wallis sat quietly observing the landscape as it went from rolling hills to flat farmland to pocosen where pine and hardwood stands are sheathed in the drapery of kudzu and all the while she was a stranger over there by the door, a passenger in the passenger seat, along for the ride with a handy guide to point the way to her lover. But I knew that bit of sarcastic fluff for what it was; for I felt not jealousy but rather an insecurity as to my place in the scope of things, and to keep from wallowing too long there I described mostly from memory the areas we drove through. At any other time, I would have stopped at Edenton. I hadn't been there in years, but to really see the old historic town you have to do more than drive through it, but who could drop from our mission to take a tour? So, I bypassed it altogether and then thumbed my nose at it from a fast-food joint on the outskirts. Nothing like a plastic lunch after hours behind the wheel, and then got behind it again for the drive up to Elizabeth City where we found first a motel and then an argument.

She claimed to have a headache and protested going onward. I said time was either wasting or of the essence which sounded like an ultimatum, and she said she wouldn't be bullied since it was her idea to come along in the first place.

So, I went off (in a huff she said) and gassed the rental and bought a map at a Shell station and then drove on up the Pasquotank (pronounced *Paspatank*) River and on out of town and soon picked up the Intracoastal Waterway and just south of the Virginia state line I came to the Dismal Swamp Canal Visitor Center. One hundred and seven thousand acres was repeated often enough that I focused on other aspects and soon learned it is the only visitor center in the country that greets visitors by both road and water, for many boats travel the waterway that stretches from New Jersey to the Gulf coast, the canal being the local stretch. I also learned of a smaller canal called a feeder ditch that connected the canal with Lake Drummond; it could be traversed by a boat small enough to portage where the ditch had silted. The Army Corps of Engineers ran an electric winch for boats under a ton, but it wasn't always operable. Well, if that wasn't more headache ammunition. Back on the highway I noticed that another road followed the southern boundary of the swamp, and so I turned there just to check it out and before long I had made a big circuit of the area, stopping several times to check the map before wending my way back to the motel. When I arrived, Wallis greeted me warmly, waved off my contrite comments and directed my attention to her laptop.

"You will recall our vexation after the poem's initial lines. While you have been gallivanting about like a cowboy, I've been studying, look here: 'an evergreen that sheds its leaves' might well be the cypress tree, see the third paragraph here, the so-named bald cypress sheds its leaves like a deciduous tree, thus naming it! Then, add the next couplet: *Yet wears a beard not French at all / In jest, say most it's Espagnol.* This has taken me the longest because I have looked too closely at the proper nouns, following leads that went nowhere affectively because I had lost myself outside the swamp. Think of trees in the Deep South, images of them, what do you see?"

"Ah, it's moss, it's Spanish moss."

"And aesthetically, a tree may be said to be bearded in that manner. In the following couplet the *wight* would support what you've told me, fantastic as it appears to be, and that will be where to find her, in a towering cypress." It was a kernel of good news, her unpacking of Charlton's taunt, but the cypress tree? At first, I was only discouraged by its ubiquity, there were sure to be tens of thousands of them, then defeated when I read of its mythical status as the symbol of mortality and of the tomb, and felt then the tendrils of a different despair, a claw tugging at my heart, one rooted in common sense and one that would surely grow until it consumed all else. Wallis appeared footloose, a didactic tease I could not bear.

"Don't look so dour Randal; we are not quite done here. Now the capital there on Time is odd—poetically it would refer to all of time—but no less so than on the determiner in the next line: This cupola, whatever could that be, I mean, why capitalize a determiner? But gee, the noun is frankly gorgeous: cupola… oh a cupola… a cupola, an appaloosa cupola," she sang.

"Wallis"

"Cupola a cupola—oh Randal, just let me go! An a cappella cupola, cupola, a cupola" and I reached for her but got breasts instead and she leaped wiggling and we fell, of course, onto the bed. I managed to calm us both down—it's all in the breathing you know, and if I must give away a trade secret, inverse syllables (but I'll hold back on the technique). Soon she was wholly herself again.

"Alright, what does alopuc do for you?"

"Spit, awful, prosaic; it's not even a word."

"Precisely that: it is not a *lexeme*. The trick is to catch it quickly. Now… as to my behavior, I am truly sorry, Dr. Fordham."

"Do you revert to the formal to cover yourself? Where are your vestments? You needn't apologize, Randal. We are adults, or are you ashamed to touch a half and half?"

"Well, I didn't mean… wasn't formulating… calming you down. And I don't think of you as other than a woman." She winked and turned back to her computer, and as I went over the syllables of her latest jag, it hit me.

From the car I got the map and back in the room I unfolded it on the bed. I had driven by it only an hour or so before and there it sat just south of the swamp: Belvidere.

"I don't see the connection," she said.

"Well, if that doesn't beat all; a belvedere is a synonym for a cupola. They've got her down there? It's not in the swamp at all, must be a dozen miles off."

"I don't believe that is it, Randal, it feels like a wrong turn."

"We're not going by feeling here. The town of Belvidere sits on the Perquimans River that flows from the swamp and the poem tells us we are looking north, so I think we begin our search there, don't you, somewhere to the north of the town and on that river."

"If you believe this to be it, you're thick as mince," she said.

"We will rent a canoe."

"Rent a canoe, rent a canoe, rent a canoe lah lah! Oh, let's rent a canoe Randal, and here's a paddle" she warbled, and made a grab at mine so hard my larynx leaped to the Geronimo response before we fell and were soon wrestling, locked together, crinkling the map beneath us, trying what wasn't clear and it didn't take, but we got the honorary pounding on the wall.

"That's not you!" I cried, rolling away.

"Randal, you know what we like."

"Stay calm, this is… we? What are you saying?" She rolled around on the map removing her blouse.

"I've got a right to verbs, mister!" Unbutton of pants. My back was to the wall.

"Could it be a subjunctive sublimate, no, no, not in a decade of subjective pining, platoons of modifiers disagree! Maybe it's the heat coupled with an absence of dynamo hum; that might be it, Wallis." She began squirming off the pants. I looked away. "Wallis, a decade of rabid nouns; defy this!"

"I'll say what pleaseth me."

"Say that again?"

"Look, look it isn't about what I say!"

"Wallis please, it matters very much to me."

"Cure me Randal, and with it the addictions."

"Stop it! Can't you see this motel has stereotyped us? We've bounced a bed and been wall pounded; we must refuse seemingly obvious conclusions!"

I left the room but the balcony was a release to nowhere, and I stormed back in to unfurled ramparts, one arm akimbo the other draping a hip as a wink caught a gawk in flight and I scurried, the aluminum door latch achieving its male and female ends.

5

The next morning was cooler but still warm for October; it was nice, reassuring even that climate change had not yet obliterated Indian summer, or guilt the face of the professional. Wallis was all business as we drove highway 17 west and followed directions to Winfall, a hamlet upstream from Hertford where we rented a small boat. The river was the color of tea and as we swept upstream, I noted the absence of banks; it looked like swamp on both sides of the river, mile after mile, monotonous amphibian geography. We motored quite a way up and around many a bend, stopping to look at big trees, before motoring on and passing under two low bridges along our way as we meandered the ever-narrowing river until it was no better than a creek and neither of us had seen anything that stood out from anything else, a thought that to a local naturalist would likely be an insult, but since Fall had not yet fallen the bald cypress trees were not yet bald. Duh! What would the naturalist have to say now? So, we turned the boat around (came about) and went back downstream. But if there was still a straw to grab at, an area naturalist might well be it.

The boat rental guy wasn't familiar with *naturalist* or happy with my explication of it but fell into easy conversation with Wallis while I stood to the side and again had that sensation that common sense would be better served elsewhere; I had seen a million cypress trees in several hours on the river, would it be any different inside the swamp, or on that feeder canal? We were merely scratching the edges, but then the boat guy said something that gave me hope:

"Wont somebody knows 'em air swamps, get Chalmers, C-h-a-l-mers. Me's your han. Got a nose he does. 'Round here he's the best find fisher."

"Fish finder, you mean?" said Wallis.

"What I said there sweetkins, his note has a bows of its own and he knows that swamp like the hack of his band. They even got him over to the college cleaching a tass. Don't know his number but you ask anyone, they'll tell you how to find the Swamp Fox."

We walked back to the car in silence.

"Randal, was he teasing us? I could not listen; I shut him off!"

"He was fairly tightlipped when we rented the boat, but somehow the name of this fish finder fellow got him pretty worked up; I have been rejuvenated, for what you just heard, or didn't, was a smorgasbord of spoonerisms. You know, transposed letters, a kind of phrasal metathesis spread across several words. Why, one of these days I will bite a rook of them. And that fellow was a natural. Let's talk to the college." And that we did.

But we detoured for lunch in Hertford where the river is estuarine before the Albemarle Sound, and the town's fine old buildings and restored colonial houses gave to it the picturesque of postcards, and a swing bridge too, said the waitress at Jakes Crab Cakes, a cheery, chatty blond eager to help the tourists.

"Lot of folks from all over come to look at these houses, take pictures you know, and that's because a lot of them are historic, you can trace them a long way back. You go down Caroline Street or Amelia and you'll see plenty and did you know George Washington stayed in a house out near Winfall? Some say it's haunted, but I know that's not true my daddy painted it last year, and I helped him and if there was a ghost I would a seen him but you should go there before you leave because, well it's a special place too you know why? It sits on a hill, and there just aren't any hills here anywhere but right there and perched right up on top as pretty as you please is the room where he stayed, George Washington I mean. Y'all want more tea?" She was back a moment later with a brochure touting historic Hertford (once home to the Algonquian Indians but chartered in 1758, we learned) that listed more than a dozen Victorian and Georgian homes and the dates of their construction. We would see many examples of these fine homes until we found ourselves in one.

At the college we made our way to the office of the registrar that directed us to Continuing Education that directed us to the Dean of Academic Affairs who said he had already said all he had to say about the issue and shut the door in our faces while sending us back to the registrar who didn't look pleased to see us again, but I beat him to the draw.

"Something tells me that Chalmers' name has changed to Mudd in the court of public opinion."

"Look, I'm sure the legislature has better things to do than send another team; everything was covered at the inquest," he said, pursing his lips. All I had said to him on our abbreviated initial visit was that we had come from Raleigh and were looking for one Wiley Chalmers, locally known as the Swamp Fox. Wallis and I exchanged glances and he read our confusion as disbelief.

"Look, the college seeks closure on this issue, so I'll be brief: as a part-time evening instructor your Mr. *Fox* got a little frisky with a coed and as a result he was placed on probationary status until the charges could be corroborated, but he surprised everyone and resigned. All attempts to contact have failed, and we have no further information." It was another dead end.

We left the office and headed to the student union where we got coffees and sat at a table facing your garden variety quadrangle. Well, now what? I brooded over the sheer volume of the swamp and its tributaries, the numbers from the visitors' center parading their immensity and volume, and then the real, the actual in the spooky cling of it that crowded around and seemed to swallow our tiny boat, all of it in a grand, sweeping denial like an outer ring of fog to mask the gloom that had begun to creep over me, a clawing despair in an opalescence of utter futility, and now this. But my thoughts rose a tad with the sense-lift that a poem had gotten me—us this far, unraveled like a rope ladder and we had climbed, had we not? Frankly, if it hadn't been for Wallis' interpretive skills, her ability to break down scansion and dissect lines and locate messages within the bottle of verse, I would be a hapless wreck. I can unscramble morphemes until the proverbial cows come home whereas Wallis could unpack verse until pastoral ruminants returned to the fold.

"Randal, I felt your spirits rise, tell me it isn't so."

Something stirred in me, instantly inappropriate yet wildly delicious, my love's lover holding my hand, may the circle be unbroken, spake the worm Ouroboros. "I guess a rebirth of hope in words, for they are what got us here," I said.

"Propelled, I think, would better articulate the matter." And she offered another smile.

"Alright, doctor tell your doctor." I smiled back, the first one in days.

"So, where are we then?"

We were facing each other as much as was doable in those awful molded chairs, and we now clasped hands.

"Well, I think we should go to the courthouse." So, off we headed for the quad and its crosshatch of walkways on our way toward the car and we passed a message board with its Jackson Pollack of stapled flyers but after a moment I doubled back. *Elizabeth City: an Historic Photographic Journey*, it read. The adjectival suffix twins snipped at me. Why not Historic Elizabeth City, or they could have made Elizabeth City possessive and done away with that silly article altogether, or why not—my grumblings interrupted by Wallis tagging a photo front and center: The Charlton-Chalmers House, and atop its mansard roof sat a cupola as pretty as you please. The exhibit would be on display in the library for the month.

"It's like we're playing detective," she said.

I felt a spring in my step.

"Talk to yourself then, see if I care."

"Giving voice to the thought process isn't as malignant as it sounds, you know."

"Depends on whose thinking you're applying words to, doesn't it?

"Oh, come on, that's just a bit Freudian for me, thank you."

"More like Jung if you think about it, no pun intended." As soon as we both shut up, the campus avian natter came alive, a language of just getting on with the day without the incessant prattle of the two-legged beasts.

6

The library was fairly small for a college but bright with large windows along two sides. We found the exhibit and its curator, a tall elderly gent in a button-down argyle.

"Ask me anything you like," he said to Wallis, with a smile more of recognition than of welcome.

"Are you a native of these parts?"

"Lived here all my life."

"Well, we're interested in this house here."

"I am surprised you haven't stopped by. You're Wallace Fordham, am I right?"

It wasn't so much that she didn't shake hands, but rather that look of startled insouciance that gave her an insubstantial sheen, like she was made of onionskin, and I recalled the motel scene. He knew her, but if rebuffed he didn't show it, but this transpired in an instant before I swept us onward.

"Are you a friend of the—" and Charlton's image caught in my throat, "owners," said Wallis, finishing it like she could read my thoughts. He walked us down to a poster sized photo of the house in panoramic view that showed a river in its frontage. He pointed.

"Had us a storm what sprung up this side and ripped some shingle, but I about got her back to right and opened up again."

"The house is… open?"

"Well sure, that tour money what doesn't go to the fund feeds me and the missus."

"You are the caretaker, then?" He offered a hand.

"Cousin on the Chalmers side." Wallis began to ask about the hyphenated surnames, but I cut her off.

"We would really appreciate a tour."

We got one two hours later when he called us at the motel and we drove on over. Far too antsy to appreciate the tongue-and-groove oak flooring and the cypress wainscoting, trappings and accouterments in gilded filigree (if a museum was animate, it'd live in a place like this), I almost floated up the stairs to the roof where the commentary about the cupola was brief.

"From up here you get the bird's eye view of our Dismal friend."

Indeed, we did, as the sun's fingers striped the foliage in a weird light partway between daylight and evening, and I grasped in a heartbeat the mythical northern light of artists, a magisterial light! We were facing north in *This cupola*! A narrow black river swept before us through patches clear of overhang and from a distant tangle, the great swamp itself. I scanned an arc with the binoculars I'd bought in our scramble for gear before the cousin had called, and then I traversed more slowly the other way and rested on a clump.

"There off to the left," I asked, "there's a clump of trees that are taller than the rest. Would you have any idea how tall they are, how far away?"

"Well sir," he said, addressing Wallis, easier on the eyes I suppose, "that there is no ordinary tree and it's not a bunch of 'em, just one mind you and bigger than ten put together."

Wallis now held the Steiner 10 x 40s to her eyes and the cousin spoke to her as though I wasn't there, guiding her elbow. "There, you see it? Known around here as the Garland Tree." I squinted to see the dark finger that rose above the broccoli fringe.

"There's something unique or very unusual about this tree," suggested Wallis.

"You musta forgot all about it." He knew her from before, but she didn't know him: most odd.

"Few ask about the Garland Tree, but I can tell you it might look burned, you can see where it's blackened, but it has lived for a thousand years and more. You can't tell from here, but it's all alone."

"How do you mean, alone," I asked. His look said this lady, not you, but he said:

"Well, it floats, got its own island, stays away from fires, things of that nature."

"But it is already burned, how did that happen," said Wallis.

"Shoot, now that story's as old as the world itself."

Here we go, I thought, as the spectral light grew fainter, shadows longer.

"Why, it was back before —but wait up a second, most folk take a quick look around and head on down. But you two wanna know about the Garland Tree; I guess that makes me curious."

"We want to go there."

"Well, that you can if you get a boat boy." I hadn't heard the comma, so I was unsure what he meant, but Wallis picked it up.

"Is there a boat rental here?" It seemed a silly question for an area laced with rivers, and hadn't she lived here with Norse as had been implied?

"I study trees," I lied, in need of a rationale, "so can you find us a boat?" I despised the craven whine in my voice, but beggars are rarely eloquent.

"You been in boats?" I told him of youthful summers on Falls of the Neuse.

"Everybody and their brother got a boat. But I'll tell you what I know," and we headed back down the stairs.

"Most scientists and naturalists say pretty much the same thing: carbon coronal discharge. I looked it up, and it means a self-sustaining spark. Shoot, they claim what makes that tree glow at night is continuous electricity, my friends, but that's not it. They're talking about St. Elmo's fire; I'm talking about St. Elmo, or maybe the angels that made him saintly in the first place. The scientists are sure of their facts, but I am sure of one thing only; that tree is the deity of the Dismal."

We spoke a while longer on the veranda beneath the massive columns and he said he would make the arrangements for a boat and that all we needed to do was motor up the main river and always aim for the widest part on account of cricks run off the channel and of course it gets scrawny pretty far up. We then followed him up the state road to a dirt track that wound through meadow to a turnaround beside the river. He'd have a boat there about ten.

I didn't sleep that night.

In the morning light we stepped over the gunnel and stowed our gear: rope, binoculars, gloves, water, a bag of apples, a bottle of bug spray, the gimme caps we had picked up at the Shell station the day before and a multi-purpose tool of a bristling Swiss utility. I stowed it under the thwarts and shoved the boat into the stream, lowered the motor and yanked the cord. We headed out onto the river, the water the color of night.

Before too long, a lack of depth perception prevented our seeing the encroachment of the banks which not unlike the Perquimans were no banks at all but a line of Black Gum, White Cedar, Cypress and Oak trees growing in the water along the edges of the channel, water that stood as the surface all around us and brackish from its ancient vast carbonaceous deposits of peat. We headed straight up the middle and kept on, moving ever closer to the tree lined edges of the murky fastness and now the channel corkscrewed and I let off the throttle and coasted because we had come to the end, but something didn't feel right, so with an oar I poled us back some ways and then came about and we headed slowly back through the curves in the direction we had come, and sure enough another channel bearing off was the right one, we would learn. I killed the motor and tossed the anchor and said we'd take a short break, have a snack. Wallis handed me the backpack and rolled overboard! My thoughts of snakes vanished when she tossed her bra, followed by her panties and a taunt.

"C'mon sugar, cool off with me, we both know you want it." I was already soaked and was considering when she dove beneath the boat but failed to surface on the other side, or anywhere. I kicked off my shoes and jumped in and thankfully there she was, submerged and treading. I eyed a white oval in the depths between the inverted V of her legs and sounded for it so fast my head entered the doorless washing machine, rusty tear ducts lining its gaping eye, and all about it other refuse lay strewn, as though the bottom was paved with aluminum. Above, Wallis' evanescent body rippled ethereal in that murky light and I wanted her then, ethics be damned, but she swam away as I approached.

When I got back in the boat, she was half-dressed and miles away, for she made no move to cover herself, didn't appear to see me at all. I got busy with the anchor rode and soon enough had us idling in the stream and it was then I noticed the wing tip of a tattoo in about the place where Claudia had a Harpy, the torso of a woman in the trunk of a vulture. I hadn't noticed it during her impromptu striptease but then who would, given the aggregate display and my scramble to vamoose. I eased us back into the channel and before long we followed no discernible track until we swept past solid banks with jungle close behind and soon after foliage scraping the gunnels and the two of us ducking low like kids, and then it opened again into a channel and that channel into a wider embowered pool, quite dark from overhang, but we were not alone. Dragonflies swarmed about us as the cousin had said the skeeterhawks would, feasting on the insects that would have made a meal of me, being a mosquito magnet from way back.

Wallis asked to steer and so we switched places and I took the forward thwart and she went aft. As we motored on, I thought of the kindly cousin and our dialogue beside the river:

"What's driving you so hard to the Garland Tree?"

"Well, first tell us why it's called that," I said.

"Okay, fair enough, most of the year it wears a skirt of hyacinth, your old lily pad of lore. Sometimes the ring is gone for a length of time but then it comes back. It's a strange thing but no stranger than the other legends that go with that tree."

"You said before that it moves?"

"That it does, indeed. I've seen it in different parts of Drummond, that's the lake, but mainly it stays in a pocosen about two miles from here, where we saw it from the roof."

"I don't see how a tree could move about and yet remain rooted." But my skepticism evaporated as I flashed on a parallel contradiction that I had recently seen with my own eyes, held in my arms, Claudia, dual-gendered and ethereal.

"Well, there is one Native legend called the deer tree that concerns one of these ancient bald cypresses on the lake; it was a deer that changed itself into a tree to escape hunters, but in another version of the tale the deer was a witch. Having changed herself into a deer and then a tree she was somehow unable to reverse the process but lives on as an immortal tree.

"And another Native legend tells of a spectral honeycomb in the crown with the dress of lilies. Every brave that climbed to retrieve the comb would return with only a crusty cone of beehive, long empty and dry as dust. Sometimes when the sun strikes the crown you can see it there winking, and at night too, catching starlight or making its own fire, but I don't believe it can be tagged as any one thing. A scientist my brother hauled out there got pretty far up and observed, so he said, nothing but the blackened core of the trunk and a smatter of St. Elmo's fire; all he got for his effort was a noggin full of bird paste. But I have my own theory."

"I would love to hear it," said Wallis who slapped at a mosquito."

"The one that got away," I said.

"You get pretty far up Moccasin Track you'll have you a serenade of skeeterhawks and won't a one of 'em bite you, regardless what you come for."

"What is Moccasin Track?"

"What that stretch of the river's called."

I knew it wouldn't mean native footwear and filed it. No use riling Wallis.

"It's the legends, really," I said. "We want to observe the tree, maybe get up in it and check it against research, compare the fantastic with the real."

"Well, here's something most folks don't get an ear of: that tree's a hybrid, perhaps the only one of its kind anywhere. To my eye it is an Atlantic White Cedar but the experts snicker and tell me it is a giant bald cypress, imply I'm too old to know Jack. White Cedars don't have knees they say; this one got knees go out forty- foot; you can look it up, but don't talk down to me. Yet, they are both conifers so it is surely possible, and out there, possibility is another realm. What the experts do agree on is its age which in turn they don't believe, either. But it *is* a cedar, a cedar with knees, and I think perhaps the longest roots, like those trees in China, forget the name, where the roots spring from the limbs and hang down like braided hair."

"Like a kite with an endless ball of string," I added, lost in dancing images of Claudia's face in the clouds where she kept reminding me of something… something important.

"Yes, sir, that is it. And I also believe that tree is maybe not a tree at all. I haven't been so foolhardy as to shinny up her with a magnifying glass like some of these mud larks, but I have sat quietly for long hours nearby and listened to her, to the wind in her hair, to her creaks and groans, and to my own heartbeat, and I sense power there."

I didn't have anything to add and Wallis, looking thoughtful, seemed to agree.

"So, you are headed for the tree and up, am I right? Get yourself two-hundred foot of half- inch rope;

I'm talkin' hemp. I've known that synthetic to granny up a square knot. Heck's Hardware, I'll give you directions."

I now grabbed that bundle of rope and put it under my head, scooted forward and hung my legs over the bow and soon, with the droning outboard….

The wooded hill stood before them sheathed in smoke as the ranks filed past and he sat his horse not his horse somebody's horse and watched them as cannon shot exploded over to his left and for a moment it worried him, shouts took his attention and they came past Elmer and the Pyrates in the front line and then the Funderbarke boys and he knew it was wrong to have a parking lot at a battle and the smoke obscured again his view and he wanted to go home but the horse went away from him and then came galloping back amid exploding shells and General Poe rode him and I too rode with the eyes of a raven… the blood caked field was strewn with bodies and parts of bodies and he walked the horse through it all, shells exploding, and toward a distant civilian: it's all gone, the harvest, my wife, my home, shot full of holes, the man said from beneath a gut shot mare clouded with flies. I asked for rope he said the barn and shells came and burst there and against the house and I found a sniper in the loft and killed him, brought the rope and hitched the hind quarters, cinched it around the pommel and dragged free the beast of burden. You're wounded said I, an arm and leg as red as the sun and when he went to wave me off fainted straight away. I cleaned and dressed him and moved him under a spreading oak, out of the shell fire and the rain of balls and he came to in there in the shade. You an officer he said and the General got an etch of himself down the ages before he gave the farmer the hardtack in his saddlebags and his canteen, and then he mounted Jenks and rode to the sound of the guns, but when the farmer cast his eye farewell, he was newly wrinkled, clean shaved, addressing a stovepipe man in a top hat who had come to admire the garden. I didn't vote for you he said and the tall man smiled. Sweet corn will do well here, it is good ground, said Abraham and pulled a sheaf from his tunic and from that foolscap; tell me if you think this sounds right, and he read. Well, I do not care for that all in there you see it is not necessary. At Seminary parse all that is not all was the rule, one I follow to this day, one you might avail of, Mr. President. The lanky Abraham sauntered to a stump and sat knees up like a daddy longlegs and wrote for a good while, carried his own ink the farmer knew, paper, printing press, disaster headlines but there they sat the two until the old copy was discarded and old Abe departed. The farmer held the discarded draft and watched him walk out of his field but saw again the rebel general who had saved his life and knew then a debt of gratitude would be paid and he too strode from the field and over the legions dead and climbed into a boat and lay down between the thwarts and with Claudia at the tiller they swept away….

I awoke pleased that Claudia had been in the dream and that I could pretend she was there behind me, guiding the boat that now slipped along through blinking shadows that lurked between trees made monstrous by their kudzu mail skirts in the brackish water, a sinister chiaroscuro amid the twisted snake-laden vines awaiting the unwary… and it gave me perverse pleasure there in the sweaty murk to aggrandize the spirit of my writing mentor and who else he may be, Dughall, Dusenburg, and how many more, and in that moment I hated him; I'd been in his story long before he had been in mine, and I had been played by a processional. Yet, I could turn it around on him if only I knew where, the how, and all the rest of it he had given me, and I was happy that I had taken his advice and kept him in the tale, the popinjay.

"Randal!"

Between my knees I saw a bank dead ahead and then we struck. I swiveled around, and with the sun in my eyes or in my stupor, Wallis shimmered, seemingly more of a wafer than wayfarer, but the motor! I shut it down and hoped we hadn't fouled the prop. Before us loomed tall grass, the kind we used to call snake grass!

"There Randal, plain as a pikestaff, it's the tree." She, not the tree, had my attention, for Claudia had oft said that; it was one of her pet expressions." She winked.

"Randal look, the tree is moving!" Across the shrub-thick bog fronting us, a bog in the fettle of man, it seemed, the tree rose columnar.

I laughed. "Ever heard of wind?" But then I woke up to the dilemma that faced us: sitting here cursing or doing something about it. It was then that I noted trash; we had wandered into a dump. Does no place sacrosanct remain, have we ruined *all*?

Portage is a noun. According to the American Heritage Dictionary it means: the carrying of boats and supplies overland between two waterways, but I'd swear it was a verb that we lugged the breadth of a liquid isthmus if you get the drift, and without the promised dragonfly friends, mosquitos formed clouds about our heads when we lifted the boat to wear it like chapeau. We got about twenty steps and Wallis sank to her knees crying she just couldn't. We rested and tried again and by this method crossed the bog and as we bled an insect breakfast that continued when I went back for the outboard and the paddles.

7

Drenched with sweat and puffy with bites we beheld a great winking pool and flopped into the drink. The tree stood fifty meters off, the trunk's rise dwarfing all else. As I snugged down the motor and restowed the gear, swarms of dragonflies did appear. Wallis said she felt faint and could she lie in the boat before we started. I too was fatigued and soon had on a fresh shirt and shorts, an apple in my mouth. I envied her as she lay still, but I pushed off the bank and paddled us across the pool, and we coasted into a slot between two of the knees. Craning my neck, I beheld an enormous spire that reached to the heavens, the Garland Tree.

"I used to climb trees," I said aloud, as though to reassure myself against an immense task come home to roost, here and now, to be put in gear and throttled up, but I was stuck in neutral, revving only a memory of the trees I clambered over as a kid, bombing crawdad creek dams and sneaking smokes, a spiral of wonder and awe, for in that very creek I had molted with Claudia, but enough of that.

The lowest limb was up twenty feet or more and trying to snag it worked me to a frazzle, the new gloves chafing. I took a break, sat down and drank some water and thought about it. I needed a weight and we didn't have one. Under the aft seat I found an old tobacco tin, and inside it a dirty rag and wrenches for the motor, I guess. With the multi-blade I sliced a hole in the gimme cap bill, took off my Nikes and packed one with the wrenches inside a sock and wedged that inside the crown and ran the rope through the clasp and the hole and half hitched it. This time I did better and on the second try the ballasted end of the rope swung over and flew down. I tied a square knot with a slip above it and cinched it and then I was on the rope and working my way up, thanking my thankless father's spirit for sentencing me to Outward Bound in those high school summers. They had us doing stuff like this on breaks.

The stout branch I hoisted up on was wide and I swung up to sit a moment, looking over the pool spread before me, one bank indistinct in hooded jungle and the other winking, water back in there, and then I turned to the trunk and climbed higher. The best way up spiraled away from the boat, but I made good progress and must have been fifty feet up when I caught sight of sparkling light, a lutescent boll above, and when I'd gotten higher still, I looked to wave at Wallis: The boat was empty! As I cried her name a choir sang out, a horn blast of choral descantation from all about me, Benedictine Nuns I would later think, within a thunderclap that knocked me from my perch and I tumbled free and hit the water going deep in the murk, and as I thrashed upward a creature grabbed me and I freaked! Thrashing and flailing entwined we hit the surface and the gooey beast I pummeled was an ichthyic eel thing, sort of.

"Randal! You came for me!" squeaked its trout like snout as it flailed with tiny hands and flopped and wiggled its slick, scaly body while I fought to get away from it and swim and all at once try to gauge what had happened; clasped in the creature's claws, I beat at it while I side stroked to the boat but was too weak to hoist myself up and over the gunnel.

"Wallis! Wallis! I yelled it again and again, and the thing still draped about me spewed a watery laugh and laid its gooey lips on my face. "It's me," it squeaked, "Randal, it's me!" Before me a likeness of Claudia's eyes and mouth emerged from the aquatic vertebrate, and smiled, its tiny hands clenched upon me.

Another thunderclap knocked my grip loose and flailing, I swallowed water before I resurfaced and saw that the tree was moving, and with it the boat, tugging at its painter that I had looped on the staub of a knee. I swam over and yanked it free, frantic to paddle out and look for Wallis, but before I could do a thing Claudia's face surfaced beside the boat, the photo bomb girl, though ichthyoid, larger now and hideously lovely, hoisted herself into the boat.

"Where is Wallis?! Where are my *clothes?*"

"Randal dear you have been inside the inside of a figment ring."

"Wha?"

The tree moved away and into a mist that blurred its dimensions.

"First, we need to get away from here. You take that paddle and we go together from different sides, like this."

Not too dumbfounded to be tickled that she thought I needed instruction, and more that she would provide it sans vetement, I yanked the motor to life naked as a jaybird in the wide daylight with a - can fish be nude? As we moved away, a scaly post-pubescent fish-girl then lay down and went to sleep curled in much the same position as Wallis had before in the stern. When the bow hit the bank, she started up, the verdigris of her epidermis less silvery, and the scales as though reduced. Further thoughts of an abandoned Wallis had vanished.

"Not this way Randal. Back up, back up, more, we go through there."

Too benumbed to do otherwise, I followed the directives of my, this fish-girl-woman-sprite-lord-knows-what-else and turned the boat into a creek no wider than the hull and we scraped through as I tilted the motor up to keep the prop free of obstruction, and she called out the course turns as though a denizen and soon the creek widened to a stream and we whisked along in a broader channel that looked much like they all had and we went onward for some time during which she never once turned to me, but then, what did I care; this thing in the boat, at once a cutaneous scaly amphibian with a human face had begun to repel me.

"Here we are," it said, as I got out the clothes I'd sweated through earlier and put them on and could have offered her the T-shirt, but what would it matter?

She had brought us out of the swamp to the branch of the Pasquotank, and she pointed: over there is your car. I couldn't see a thing except the river, the Moccasin Track. She made to get out of the boat.

"Claudia—whoever you are, don't, this place is known for poisonous snakes!"

"Oh laddie," she said with a laugh, "after all we have been through," and she dove in only to reemerge larger, more hominoid, wearing a soggy mass of reedy green hair and she sagged over the gunnel in a heap, saying she was weak. Then another surprise when she whispered:

"Your family papers, tell me, are they safe?"

The facsimiles, the originals, snug as a bug: you wouldn't believe how safe they are, before the thought process leaped from the Raleigh manse and its trunk to the trunk of the rental, by now broken into, trashed or hauled off to an impound yard? I lurched with a leg cramp and leaned over to massage it and then got one in the other leg and writhed, supine beside a lovely woman I didn't want any more, in whatever form, whatever motion; I had rescued a succubus, but I must have been muttering.

"I merely steered from within, dear boy; I saw and steered thee and wore the form, but she was hard Randal, her bag in transition, you must help me… we are in grave danger."

She lapsed again into unconsciousness, and I could not rouse her. I rolled her over and beheld up close those scaly impressions intaglio upon her flesh, and though repelled I tried to caress her, but she was cold, cold everywhere I lay my hands. Whatever she had become opened an eye for a moment and said, "We will meet him there." And whatever I had become was too tired to care which adverb she meant, and the direct object could go fuck itself, for the journey into and out of the swamp had taken—wait a second, my watch said that two days had passed; time to dump this cheesy chronometer, and I wondered if they made a multi-tool with a clock.

She did not awaken for another full hour, the sky paling about us when at last she arose. Without a word we made for the opposite bank in the crepuscular gloom. But it was there beside the softly gurgling river that I learned anew about life and about love, and though I had always been morally certain and ethically correct in the application and the exercise of the Golden Rule, it didn't stick as well as I believed in that moment it would, for events would sweep it from my grasp.

We tied off the boat and as I wolfed trail mix, I noted that she had mostly reclaimed her shape, though her dorsal fin was smaller now. I sat on a thwart and appraised her. Before going any further, I had to get some things off my chest.

"I was so worried, distraught, where you had been taken by them." She squeezed my ankle.

"Oh Randal, it wasn't me that went away, it was you."

"They put you inside that ball." I thought of it in my pack, some dimensional game piece.

"That is what seems to happen. Since the auction we have both been transported by the Mirln Domhanda, but I have been able to project through you the reality you lived, thank Titania, that led to my own freedom, and now to yours, but we are still in danger."

She was uttering nonsense, and trying to make sense of it made my head swim as I shook it.

"A figment ring, Randal… the inside of the inside is like the outside but… it's not exactly that, and that's where you were. Within the Domhanda alone naught would have transpired. I would have been a prisoner in that realm you know as a tree for all of Time, which itself would unravel at Hyperbole's hand and doom for all would have ensued."

Figments indeed! "Look, it wasn't a dream, I saw and lived everything, did everything actual, *real*, Claudia, not an act."

"Yes, lovely, but real is rings within rings and the inside of the inside is a mirror to you."

"I never saw myself! No, but rather, everything I saw and did lead me here to you." I could argue this one all day.

"Not yourself but of yourself, your conscience, your actionable thoughts Randal, your desires and your love brought our rings into alignment." She kissed me, but I ducked most of it.

"But how— no, wait a minute… how did I get the Domhanda? I got it from that detective, I've had the marble and I brought it along in my pack. I don't know why, it just seemed connected to all this."

"Each step took you closer, from your ring to mine and we are free, for now, but we must move quickly before they find the documents."

"The documents are over there in the car, locked in the trunk."

"Shh! Do not speak it, do not even think it! Prevent the entry. Do you not see we're released from the rings, but time is mathematic, Randal, and you are nigh blind to it."

In the space of a twitch, she straddled me, "come along," and wrapped around her we lay together on a bed of air *and all about me an opaline iridescence shimmered and eddied but growing fainter as though we traveled upward through a cone of light and at its apex a murky vaulted room where from above, I saw Wallis at her table amid illuminated manuscripts and books and beside her a steaming mug of tea. I spoke to Claudia, beside me there, yet not.*

"But I knew Dr. Fordham long before we met."

"She is quite real, and it's why I brought you hence. I merely borrowed her spectral form and projected into it, for she, after all, was without and you and I within. Additional weight of task to project you as well, dear boy, and in so doing I was far too busy to haunt you in the Mirlin, though as our paths crossed, the more frequently and readily I worked, I sensed that we would lock and meet as we did, but thou hath weathered my form," she said, and we were back in the boat, or I was, for she rolled overboard again and I swore I heard murmuring water as I sat in the failing light before she reappeared, smaller now but greenish again, slumped against the gunnel. She stirred and I reached to check for pulse; she had none but was enlivened at my touch.

"Projecting the both of you synchronic hath worn through me, and for it I have begun to wear away, a diminishment I cannot forestall the longer I retain this human shell." She didn't speak more and I sat and looked at her, again mixed as before, the grand plan of ditching her too palindromic in its message. But I too was tired, more than I could remember being, and so decided to move the boat closer to the car instead of walking fifty feet. The trusty motor kicked to life and the boat glided up to the bank where my car was guarded by a shotgun-wielding Norse Charlton.

"The love birds at last," and he pointed the ugly end at me, and too worn to tear my eyes from its menace jones, I stared into binocular death.

"What we need is to get rid of lover boy here, the problem child. First, he opens the car and gets what we need."

"We shan't, for presently we are no more, nor shall we be," whispered the clump of a rag doll Claudia, trying to raise herself. Charlton thumbed the hammers.

"Okay, okay." I arose and my wooden legs again seized in both calves, and I screamed and tumbled overboard where I flopped in agony in the shallows and Charlton loomed, menacingly.

"Well Randal, I must say you are as daft as a brush, and in more ways than one. Certainly, we told you about introducing characters at the end of a tale, the novice knack for lack of talent to carry the action forward on its own, but here you are with that cousin, a chap who, by the way, would like to thank you."

The cousin stepped from the grass and walked over, crossed behind Charlton, flickered and appeared again as an iridescent Mrs. Dusenburg, a shade lighter than a shade, and the two of them stood there, a pair of orgulous grandees, before the lady seemed to fold, dropping in a clump in the shallows by the boat, as though abandoned by the puppet master.

I had a spark: the mirlin domhanda was in my pack and Claudia knew how to work it, if we could get Norse–wait a second, what had he said, new characters, and when he chided me about abandoning them, and that's when it hit me. When I regained my feet in the shallows and faced him, the shotgun flew from his hands and splashed amid the moccasins and he duck marched into the boat. Claudia had raised herself, almost whole again but for the tail fin.

"Welcome back to the story, Norse, and the wee folk it's been about all along."

"Randal, what are… no! You cannot do this!" Smaller already, he too dwindled.

"Oh, but I can, and let us recall the one that showed me the how of it all."

"Listen to me you fool; we both know your tale is ending! Inserting me as another character is not merely bad form—haven't I taught you anything? It is utterly pointless! Look, *all* we want is that one word and we'll be gone."

"You, uncle," mumbled Claudia, and as she grew Charlton shrank away, to be winnowed for his new role, "you alone."

I was too wiped out to keep all the shape-shifting straight as to who was the uncle, but I inched him forward another couple steps until he cried:

"The *all*, it is the *all*, oh please, please us, it is *all* we ever wanted," he pleaded.

"Claudia, shouldn't he be on his knees for this?"

"Absolution time or story time" she sang as she lay back against the hull, finless now, leggy. Charlton found his ability to genuflect athwart of Claudia's knee, though he struggled.

"It began with Erasmus," he mumbled.

"Shut it," cried Dusenburg, sprawled against the bow and beside Claudia, and in a like state.

"We will to ash and dust, endless this match cannot be," said she.

"Aye, but shadows pass."

"He cannot be worth the greater value lost," she said, eyeing me.

"Randal: you, all of your kind had a pixie form, but have long forsaken your will to shift—once you could do it in spite of the consequences, but so thoroughly abused the privilege you morphed into the lard bags you now trudge about; be thankful, but for that, you would see all."

I wanted Norse's story, but the value remark cheapened it.

"What consequences?"

"Oh Randal, haven't you noticed at all how I am after a shift? You don't pay attention to me; you don't even *see* me when I am whole; you take me for granted when otherwise I am not greater than a figment!"

I sat on the gunnel and she slapped my face just as Wallis had!

"Two sides Randal, we have them and always shall; one of you brings me great pleasure and a fulfillment I haven't before known, but this other, Randal, no listen to me, of this other I believe you are in the wrong field. The checkerboard needs you over there with the writers, the creative block; you went down this counseling path because it felt right, a salve to your system but it is not where you belong, really.

"This horrid thing, my uncle's lover-slave is on to you, he sees what I see in a broader reach, dear boy. Randal, when we take human form there are too many luscious flavors and we easily get stuck in the nectar that enticed us in the first instance; the attractions are too dear. How Dughall got from Aristotle to Pliny and then all the way to Shives Poe, you tell me, you were treating him."

Dusenburg spoke as though from sleep: "Human form hath spun me down like a whirligig, and ever the more I change, the weaker I become; my spirit is but a balloon, and I fear it drifting ever after, but therein lies the answer; I must fly!"

"Hype, you enlivened the age you carried; laurels await but honor bestowed upon a crust is no honor at all. Come with me, let us to home."

I couldn't follow these leaps from shape shifting to career counseling, and picked up the earlier thread:

"Erasmus, Norse, I don't give a damn about him, you scoundrel. Having inserted you, I see that your insidious history will be a drawback; I think Claudia is right."

"No! Oh Gorgon, I swore I'd whistle thy name down the spiraling air in Domhanda, with you in gaol forever; but here you are again! you mewling clotpole, curse thee!"

He spun to confront her and the two of them set to arguing so furiously it was all I could do to keep him in the boat part of the chapter that I was furiously inventing when the Claudia I well-remembered struck, slapping him so hard a grape-sized gobbet shot forth and she snagged it like a shortstop.

"Well, the Domhanda indeed, you worm! A moment gone you had me but spun out by the presence of this dear mortal, sacrosanct to you and me, where you'd have kept me, I will now keep you."

"If that's the Domhanda, then what's this," I said, removing the marble from my daypack.

She chirped: "The Cyclic! Aye, it guided you Randal, a steering of scope, it helped you locate the portal, only you did not carry it, Hah! It only seems that way; it carried *you* here, aligned the rings that held us. I bade you steal it from that sleeper who stole it from me, yet I had him dwell as an idiot. So, have I them once again as it is meant to be; a set, they are, a bolt and its wheel. Time is wasting Norse!"

As though afraid to look her in the eye he grew smaller still, conforming to his role as one that diminishes by shades.

"Okay look it was the *all*, all of them, every all, don't you see, stealing from the polymaths, polymaths, polymaths, stealing from the polymaths is all we love to do! But Erasmus was so dull, you see, his *alls*, we took more than one, he-he, but they meant so little compared to his evermore elite contemporaries, Leonardo, and then Copernicus, Michelangelo, Newton, now those *alls* had power! But we have taken *all* from quadrants across the ages because it got us high, the ripple over Time, it was grand enjoyment dipping onto pages and getting a lovely buzz, and let me say here and now leaded ink is one thing you *people* have ruined, Randal"—he swiped at me, lost his balance, and fell between the thwarts. Gunless he was fighting me yet, the rotten bastard. I made him shorter still, the easier to arise and speak once again, and rotely:

"You can never take enough all for it *all* to be over."

"You contradict yourself, and what's any of this got to do with me?" The look he gave, as that to a dismissive child, a minikin curtsy with knitted brows and that sleepy half-lidded effect of the crocodilian, answered the question.

"In that time, the power of oratory far outranged the pen," he squeaked, resistant to the role designed, but giving is a different character trait than drawing, and I needed him to enlarge upon his theme and warm to its expanse, and so I was pondering his role when Claudia spoke.

"Bollocks!"

She was full again, all female but a wafer-thin waif, and I stared like a penitent, and with my attention drawn he scratched and gnawed the way characters do that you know aren't a good fit for the role — "ouch, you asshole!"

"We have the Marble, not you," said Claudia.

"Dare not cousin," he hissed.

"*Worm*, you cannot appreciate the nature of what you are, and where tell are we now?"

"Right back where we—you started. I am so tired of this insult… I will not lose to *you*! You and this unmuzzled onion-eyed skainsmate you're shagging. Pog mo thoin!"

Wearier than a dead horse flogged, I snapped, and Charlton was reduced to about the size of a four-year-old and now Claudia loomed, rolling the marble on her palm, and as I loomed too, the weight shift ballasted the empty tobacco can.

"Here's the deal Charlton: you tell me about my life, my—*your* interdiction and my place within it, or you're going in that can!"

Claudia disagreed (with the logic of a fish) and we huddled aft for a stern discussion: "Randal, can you not grasp what has been? Hyperbole has spun you like a top, yet you revolved while the orbit remained; figments have appeared as people, entered your life, interacted with you, and when their purpose was fulfilled, they exited as though they never were; I warned you before that Dughall and this worm here were playing you, but you didn't listen; truth told, you haven't listened very well at all to what I have had to say to you: your ideals of princely love have sealed your ears."

Well, the more I learned, the more I spluttered sloppy sentences and so felt the rising challenge of my writing teacher's rage and knew he was no whipped puppy, but that wasn't the challenge I needed to face just then, one that had already moved on. Claudia wanted him, both of him I would guess, ensconced in the domhanda, a secure place in which to wallow within the corridors of Time's detention center, yet cause no mischief, but I parried, too weary to follow (her meaning) and far too tired to do much more at all when the kid tried to bolt! Before he could hop out, I surged up from jerry-rigged umbrage and off the cuff winged a stellar paragraph that made him the size of an airline shot of Scotch and rolled him into the tobacco tin and closed the lid. You got Prince Albert in the can?

"You let me out of here," he pealed. At the gunnel I scooped river water into my mouth, and splashed it all over me and it revived me enough to continue scripting his lines.

"Alright then, it was after we hit Benjamin Franklin, ring a bell, and what a lovely man was he, fat with ideas, a Leonardo of light, a key holder; we felt at home in his home in the new nation and decided to stay on, and hey what's an eon or two, but onward we could see that Lincoln was slated for the apex, the balance, the culmination, the very acme of *all*; and to that end we moved, but failed to account for a venomous vocabulary otherwise unknown to us, and it threw the project to the wrench.

"To that moment you people had not been set as free as we had measured, and we saw that word as the ultimate *all* to achieve, building as we had been all the while, taking *all* from kings abreast the wash of it all and we rode the waves, so wild and free the ripples across time."

Claudia shook her head at the pride in his eyes.

"Those ripples would have destroyed everything you know, Randal," she said. "I have spoken all of this before; I have kissed it into you; I had your ear in dream flight and o'er many a field instructed you, and also how many times in that dreadful plastic cell you call a living room! Have you heard me at all? It was I alone put those morphemes back, each and every *all* while the only flux these minnows rode upon was the wake created by their own self-delusion."

I peered into the can at the man with the tiny tan underwear lines and giggled, that is until I choked on a memory, or was it that?

"Wait a second, what about my grandfather?

She stilled my lips. "Your Shives Poe, dear boy, met a young maiden in the forest of the many fires, did he not, and is that not written in those papers as well? They were after it all, all of it, all of you."

"I need more," I said, as something big buzzed my head in the gloaming, fucking bugs.

"Listen to me, and then release me," shouted the defiant tiny, "the Gettysburg Address gave on a luminary reading luminaria: the greatest' *all* by its context of any all across the ages, and we had to have it! Yet, listen to me *boy*, the known copies were sequestered, sealed away, but your grandfather had a draft, a standout copy unreported unfiled unknown, except in faerie, and you very nearly forfeited it to us, but Roi will get it from you still, you paltry cur!"

My grandfather was fey? Is that what they were saying? And who's Roy? The buzzing came again, louder now, and I craned my neck in the failing light and scanned the night sky looking for what—Dusenburg had vanished.

Claudia hugged me. "He is about, but in our tussle, I pinched him just there," but my raised hand stopped her just short of demonstrating. "He will need respite surely. Meanwhile, what shall we do with this nasty little quarter man?"

Was she surrendering her prisoner? I was too tired to string one thought to another, and I could feel him grow against my uncertainty toward his character; such bases I should have had in place, he would have said; he could pop out at a moment's notice, change to some other character or fly away like the turbo-bird that was buzzing us, the uncle or his other half? She read me like a book.

"Adopted and endowed with dust is he, an amoebic flint, rather like a pocket," said she before grabbing my hair in one hand and my balls in the other and ramming her tongue down my throat and as I grew avast of her, she flipped over the gunnel and with a splash was gone in the dark water, swift as a wink, and she remained out there, out on the outside long enough for me to sense its fullness, as well as my own empty response; she was gone forever, or as she'd have put it, did a Lord Lucan.

It was full night and mosquitos hungered. Zombie-like, I emptied the boat, turned it over with the motor underneath, and with collected gear I trudged my way to the car in the star-lighted dark where I put Charlton into a deep slumber and, stretched across the back seat, followed soon after. At some ghastly hour, who knew how much later, I awoke with leg cramps, and thought wretched things: I didn't want to be saddled with an unsavory character that I would have to maintain, the cheesy bastard. Further, I didn't know how long he would keep, and while pet stores have developed their tasty treats, it seemed so distastefully cruel. After washing down some acetaminophen and waiting on the muscles to relax, I drove back to the motel for an overdue head bang with Morpheus.

8

The New York I left was wholly different from the one I returned to: time had shifted in my absence, and I found myself on the outside looking in. I knew I was professionally ruined; I had willingly led a patient into a quagmire and lost her; but that was contradicted by recent voice mail, and when at last I called her back, I was informed by the English Department secretary that she was presenting a paper at the University of Heidelberg. The relief I felt was palpable on the one hand and frightening on the other: either I had to accept Claudia's version of events or admit to lunacy. Second, having got wind of my trip south with a patient and demanding receipts for each and every hour, The Duck had fanned the flames and my chairmanship of the national association was surely tarnished, unless I stuck around to fight him and set things right, but his chicanery couldn't have stopped an invitation that had been in the mail while I chased an eidolon.

Asia's annual Language in Therapy Conference had selected me as keynote speaker, so I'd soon be off to Cebu City, in the Philippines, where Melody, incidentally, would present. Well! Things were looking up on the tail of a disastrous love affair in which the loser became the winner after all, for what I had *lost* was something I could never explain, much less understand; how love had been seduction's manufacture and lust but its gear grease, and that I had bedded and yearned to wed an Ogygian hermaphroditic amphibian with a zoo of personalities, and that was only for starters. No, I was going to file that one edgewise, a mere footnote in a serial drama.

The story I wrote for the former Norse Charlton was a pastiche of Alexander Dumas and Stendhal and Arturo Perez-Reverte in which our nasty little bandit has at last been cornered and caged and will languish in his cell, singing vowels for his dinner, alive, alive oh. And by the way, I said to him, as a thunderbolt to an ant, the cousin (or was he the uncle?) wasn't the last character in this tale, that role belongs to you, along with your new name Tom, Tom Thumbprint that is, the mightiest stentorian venter of vowels the age will come to know. I figured he would keep on tidbits until the coffers were stuffed, only then would I consider his denouement, perhaps a generation of homunculi. To date, each meal's peal has been slightly different and I had recorded them all. The MP4 insert in every can of vowels would play at the flick of a switch. So far, so good; Lyfe and I had worked out amenable terms, but he balked at aluminum.

"We want to make money; plastic is way cheaper, not to mention ubiquitous."

"And that is precisely why we won't use it; I can't believe you'd say such a thing."

"Look Poe, the less we spend the more we make, it's a simple recipe."

"I understand that, but plastic doesn't biodegrade, it photodegrades, where its polymer chains break down into ever smaller pieces that attract chemical poisons. Want more ubiquity? Something like a trillion shopping bags get manufactured annually. Daily, shipping fleets and navies jettison more than a half million plastic containers overboard. Asian island shores are littered with trash, most of it plastic, and The Philippines, where I'm headed for a conference, throws mountains of trash in the sea while being in receipt of tons of it on its beaches, and primarily it comes from us; I won't be a part of it. We go with tin or we don't go at all."

He shook his head and tried another angle.

"If we keep this thing going, it could fund our grandchildren's children, all richer than classical gods."

"A pantheon of ghouls, you mean, churners of the cyclone of polystyrene. The Great Pacific Garbage Patch is a horror story of mammoth proportions, Lyfe, we add new chapters unabated, but it isn't fiction. It is time for each of us to make a stand; we might save ourselves after all."

"Okay, okay so we'll have, say a tab activated aluminum cylinder but that MP4 seems limited. I think maybe a zigabyte chip, no over the horizon upgrades."

"Leave that to me; I've thought it through." For I knew something he did not: Tom Thumbprint was going to sing, sing, and sing for All Time, and to be for *all* seasons a mockingbird.

The End

About the Author

After graduating high school, other than a brief stint at Naropa Institute to study poetry with luminaries of the Age, Steven Mooney was for twenty years an unskilled blue-collar laborer working as a custodian, garbageman, groundskeeper, librarian, messenger, seasonal firefighter, taxi/truck driver, and also working at construction sites and factories, earning just enough money for the books he devoured across the breadth of English and American literature. Tiring of the shanty life at thirty-eight, he ventured to college and earned a Bachelor of Art in English, and a Master's in Education where he first encountered ESL. For the next twenty years he taught English in Central America, The Far East, and the Middle East, then retired to the Pacific Northwest, USA, where he lives with his wife. He is the author of *In Cellophane of Time, Poems 1973-1987*; *Kottke Ouevre Skookum, 6 and 12-string ears, Vignettes 1970-2019*; and the comic literary novels: *Cutlass Wonders*, *The Ageless of Aquarius*, and *Chronicle of an English Morpheme Addict* published under the series title: *A Measure of Poe & Three Quarters*.

www.ingramcontent.com/pod-product-compliance
Lightning Source LLC
LaVergne TN
LVHW050958080826
845145LV00009B/2346

* 9 7 8 1 7 3 4 5 3 5 6 8 6 *